6/09

Caught Between the Pages

Also by Marlene Carvell:

SWEETGRASS BASKET

WHO WILL TELL MY BROTHER?

Caught Between the Pages

marlene carvell

DUTTON CHILDREN'S BOOKS

DUTTON CHILDREN'S BOOKS
A division of Penguin Young Reader's Group

Published by the Penguin Group
Penguin Group (USA) Inc., 375 Hudson Street, New York, New York 10014, U.S.A. •
Penguin Group (Canada), 90 Eglinton Avenue East, Suite 700, Toronto, Ontario, Canada
M4P 2Y3 (a division of Pearson Penguin Canada Inc.) • Penguin Books Ltd, 80 Strand, London
WC2R 0RL, England • Penguin Ireland, 25 St Stephen's Green, Dublin 2, Ireland
(a division of Penguin Books Ltd) • Penguin Group (Australia), 250 Camberwell Road,
Camberwell, Victoria 3124, Australia (a division of Pearson Australia Group Pty Ltd) •
Penguin Books India Pvt Ltd, 11 Community Centre, Panchsheel Park, New Delhi - 110 017, India •
Penguin Group (NZ), 67 Apollo Drive, Rosedale, North Shore 0632, New Zealand
(a division of Pearson New Zealand Ltd) • Penguin Books (South Africa) (Pty) Ltd,
24 Sturdee Avenue, Rosebank, Johannesburg 2196, South Africa •
Penguin Books Ltd, Registered Offices: 80 Strand, London WC2R 0RL, England

The publisher does not have any control over and does not assume any responsibility for
author or third-party websites or their content.

CIP Data is available.

Published in the United States by Dutton Children's Books,
a division of Penguin Young Readers Group
345 Hudson Street, New York, New York 10014
www.penguin.com/youngreaders

Designed by Liz Frances

Printed in USA   First Edition

ISBN 978-0-525-47916-1

1 3 5 7 9 10 8 6 4 2

To the students at S-E

Caught Between the Pages

Chapter One

"Barnes," a voice hollered from the end of the hall. "You're headed in the wrong direction."

I didn't have to look to know who it was. Brian Carson. All-around jerk and know-it-all. You know the type. Big mouth. Full of himself. Thinks he owns the world because he's captain of the soccer team.

"Hey, Barnes," he yelled again, "we got practice."

I ignored him. It was the fourth time in two weeks I had to stay after school for my English teacher. I sure didn't need him on my case, too.

Too late. I was just about to open the door to Mrs. Jordan's classroom when his arm flew in front of my eyes as he pressed his hand against the door frame, blocking my way. Whew! No question what had been on the lunch menu. Pepperoni roll.

"Where ya goin'?" he barked at me. "You miss another practice and you're gonna be off the team."

"I gotta stay after for Mrs. Jordan," I mumbled. "I'll be there later."

"Just don't be too late," he snapped. "If you're gonna be part of the team, then you better be committed."

Threat? Pep talk? It didn't matter. He was a jerk. I wanted to tell him so. I wanted to tell him his breath smelled. But I also wanted to stay alive.

"Tell Lockwood I'll be there sooner or later."

I shifted my backpack from one shoulder to the other as I reached for the doorknob.

"Well, it better be sooner than later," he ordered as he tapped the end of his index finger repeatedly on my right shoulder.

That did it! He bullied everybody, and I was sick of it. I swung around and smacked my backpack into his stomach. Not my brightest move.

"Hey, you puny, little . . ."

I was doomed. He was a jerk, but he was also a lot taller and fifty pounds heavier than me.

Suddenly the classroom door swung open, and there was Mrs. Jordan, one hand on the knob, the other pressed against the door frame. Brian dropped his arm and backed away slightly.

"PJ, aren't you supposed to be in here?"

She paused. Then her eyes shifted from me to Brian. "Isn't there somewhere you're supposed to be, Brian? Practice, maybe?" Her voice was quiet, but the tone said for me to get in the room and for Brian to get lost. For chrissakes. Who did she think she was? I could handle my own battles.

4

"Sorry, Mrs. Jordan, I didn't know PJ was supposed to be with you. I was just reminding him we had practice." It was a typical Brian Carson suck-up. His voice oozed more honey than you find in a beehive. What an asshole.

"I'm sure PJ knows when practice is. He'll be there as soon as he can," she said as she peered over her glasses and stepped backward so I could enter the room. Maybe she had overheard our conversation in the hall. Maybe not.

Without another word, she closed the door behind me and headed toward her desk, her shoes clicking on the tile floor. Her classroom was long and narrow, and her desk was on the opposite wall from the door, near the windows. If she wanted me to follow her over there, she was out of luck. I plopped down into the desk closest to the door.

"Soccer practice isn't supposed to start until three-thirty," she began. "Let's see. Why don't you do the vocabulary test you missed first? If you don't finish the other assignments by four, you can go to practice and come in again tomorrow." She was almost to her desk when she stopped and turned back to face me. "Unless perhaps you decide to accept the idea that homework is indeed just that . . . *home* work."

"I know what homework is, Mrs. Jordan. I'm not stupid."

"I know you're not, PJ, but you have a choice. You can either do your homework at home or you can do it here. The school year has barely started, and you're digging a big hole for yourself. At this rate, you and I will be . . ."

Oh, puhleeze . . . shut up. Somebody was always telling me what I was supposed to do. Did she ever think maybe I had other things on my mind?

". . . together again next year and I—"

"Could I just take the damn test?"

She stopped talking. I didn't dare look at her. A million seconds of silence went by.

"Is something wrong, PJ?"

What's wrong? I'm sitting in a classroom after school making up work I didn't want to do in the first place instead of being at practice where the coach'll give me hell because I'm late and the captain, major suck-up and all-around bully, makes my life miserable. And she wants to know what's wrong. I wouldn't even be on the soccer team if Heather hadn't dumped me for some computer geek just before school started. Six months. Going together almost six months, and two days after this nerd moves into her neighborhood, we're through. Says their minds are in tune. In tune with what?

"Nothin'," I mumbled.

She heaved a sigh and turned to pick up something from her desk.

"It's a vocabulary test, PJ, and it sounds like maybe a little improvement in your vocabulary is warranted." She plopped two pieces of paper in front of me.

"Make sure you do both sides."

I whipped through that test. I'm a lousy student. I admit it. But I am a good reader and vocab comes easy. All the while I worked on the test, Mrs. Jordan was writing stuff on the board. Only once or twice did I see her glance in my direction. Yet she knew exactly when I was done.

"Finished, PJ?"

"Yes, Mrs. Jordan," I replied with mock sincerity as I waved the completed test out in front of me. It had been simple, and I was sure I had aced it. Clearly I didn't need to do homework to do okay. Teachers are always making you do stupid things. You know how it is. School has nothing to do with real life. It's just a plot to make ours miserable.

"Can I go now?"

She glanced at the clock as she plucked the test from my hand and dropped it on the table behind her.

"I'll compromise," she said as she set two green sheets of paper on my desk. "I want you to finish these two worksheets now. When they are done, you can either stay and do some more of the work you owe or take the rest of the materials home for homework." She emphasized the word *home* again.

I looked at the clock. It was already 3:25.

"I'll be late to practice."

"Mr. Lockwood will understand."

"I doubt it," I muttered.

I really did doubt it. Lockwood was not about to make English class more important than soccer.

"When those two assignments are finished, you may go, but not before. I'll send Mr. Lockwood a note tomorrow so that he knows you were with me."

"He won't care."

"Maybe not. But I will send him the note anyway."

I stared at the worksheets. One was on the play we were reading in class, A *Midsummer Night's Dream*. The other looked like some grammar stuff. Boring. I took a pencil back out of my backpack and started to work.

By 3:40, the two papers were finished, at least as much as I could do. I don't pay much attention in class, so some of the questions didn't make a lot of sense. Neither did my answers.

"I'm done," I announced.

"Put them in the homework folder, please." She was back at the chalkboard.

I hopped up quickly, dropped the two papers into the plastic folder that hangs on the wall just inside the door. At least I didn't have to worry about her looking at them right then.

"Can I go now?" I asked as I threw my pencil into the side opening of my backpack.

"In a minute, PJ." She stopped writing on the board and stepped toward her desk as she continued talking. "You still owe several assignments. If you want to go on to practice now, you may, but you do need to take these items with you." She scooped up a stack of materials from her desk.

"You probably won't be able to finish all these assignments tonight," she continued as she headed toward me, "but you ought to be able to do most of them before the end of the week. At the very least, I expect the assignments with a check at the top to be finished by Thursday afternoon. We will reassess what needs to be done at that time." She sort of waved the pile in front of me as though I hadn't seen it and then placed it on the desk where my backpack lay on the seat.

She just didn't get it. I wanted to pick up the pile and throw it to the floor and yell, *I DO NOT DO HOMEWORK!*

But I didn't. Instead, I slid the papers into my backpack and slung it over my shoulder as I headed for the door. I just wanted out of there. Her voice followed me as I left the room.

"Good-bye, PJ. Thank you for coming in this afternoon."

Like I had a choice?

Chapter Two

Fifteen minutes later I was running laps around the field. Late to practice. Again. Where I had been didn't matter. Mrs. Jordan's note to Coach tomorrow wasn't helping me today.

"C'mon, Barnes, let's see some hustle. You play on my team, you go by my rules."

Okay, Loudmouth Lockwood, I thought. *Maybe it's time to quit playing on your team.*

I had tried out for the soccer team only because I thought the guys would like me better. Girls, too, I thought. Maybe Heather dumped me for the nerd, but most girls like the jocks. Anyway, it wasn't working. And it probably killed any chance of getting Heather back. When she heard I was going out for the team, she just shook her head and said, "You got to be kidding." I wasn't sure what that was supposed to mean. I wasn't that bad at it. Even

9

Lockwood said I had potential. But he wanted more than I was willing to give, I guess.

So there I was on the team. Potential? Maybe. Playing time? Not much. Friends? Some. Girls? Nope.

"Okay, team, let's gather round here. If we're gonna beat Preston Thursday night, I gotta see more action than I am right now. You gotta put some hustle into every move. You gotta think Win! Win! Win!"

By this time, he was yelling. Of course he yelled all the time, so nobody listened any more than they ever did. Somehow he seemed to think we would get better just by telling us to get better. He said soccer was a mental game. The bruises on my legs said otherwise. If I got kicked one more time by one of my own teammates, I would quit.

"And you guys gotta play together! You're a team! You have to think team! *T-E-A-M!*" He shouted out each letter and then stepped back and lifted both arms upward as though he were holding a very large book in front of him.

"So, what are you?"

"A team," we responded flatly.

"You look like a team, but you don't act like a team," he yelled. "What ARE you?"

"A TEAM," we all shouted back. Just tell him what he wants to hear.

He slapped one hand against the other. He's the only person I know who gives himself high fives.

"All right! That's what I wanted to hear."

Bingo.

He was right about one thing. We sort of looked like a team.

At the beginning of the season, Brian Carson suggested we all bleach our hair. He said it would show Coach we were serious. We went along with the idea but not for the same reason. Most of us just thought it would be cool. So one night after practice when Billy Jackson's mom was working late at the hospital, we all went to his house, where his sister, who studies cosmetology at the vocational school, put her education to use. Five hours and four pizzas later, we all emerged with various shades of blond hair, some more green or orange than blond. The next afternoon at practice, Coach was so moved that he didn't yell for at least fifteen minutes. That was pretty amazing.

"Hey, PJ."

I glanced over my shoulder just as Henry Rose poked me in the ribs. That was Henry's standard hello. It was annoying, but he was harmless.

"Can you come over tonight? I need some moral support."

This was a first. Nobody ever needed me for anything. Well, I guess that's not quite true. Heather used to say that if it wasn't for me, she couldn't possibly cope from one day to the next with her family. I guess Nick the Nerd is helping her cope these days.

"You need me? What kind of moral support are we talking about here?"

"I'm changing math courses. That is, if my dad will let me. Take something a little easier. No point in killing myself over numbers. I've been trying to convince my dad for three weeks to sign the add/drop paper. If I don't do it this week, it'll be too late."

Henry was pretty cool. And most of the time he made sense, but I still wasn't sure what he wanted from me.

"So where do I fit in?"

"My dad's easier to deal with if he's in the public eye."

"So why me?"

"Billy can't come over."

That explained it. Billy Jackson and Henry Rose had been friends forever, at least long before they started letting me hang around with them. Not that they didn't like me. I'm pretty sure they did. But when Henry got to choose a friend to go to Six Flags with him every summer, I can tell you it sure wasn't me. And when Billy had to choose between me and Henry for a lab partner, he didn't hesitate for a second.

"What about Monica?" That was Henry's girlfriend.

"If it was just my mom, maybe. Dad? Not a chance."

"C'mon, guys, two more laps before you head home." That was Coach's routine. "Do it in under two minutes and no laps for you tomorrow." Like that was even possible?

Henry and I trotted off together, side by side, at the back of the group. Billy was already at the head of the pack. He was a pretty good runner. He even liked it.

"He still grounded?" I asked.

Henry nodded.

Billy's mom was not very happy about the whole hair thing. It might have been because Billy looked pretty awful, but I think it was mostly the mess we'd left at the Jackson house.

"Billy figures he's grounded until he's thirty-five. His mother claims the bathroom sink is permanently stained, and Billy says every time she brushes her teeth she adds a couple days to his jail time."

Henry was already breathing hard. He was in worse shape than I was. I'm not sure why he was on the team either. Probably because Billy was. At least Billy's mom let him stay on the soccer team, which was pretty iffy for a while, considering it was the soccer team that caused the mess. It might have been because she found out it was Brian Carson's idea, and even a parent knows he's a jerk. Of course Billy's sister wasn't blamed for her part. Girls never are.

"Well? Can I count on you, PJ?"

I think it was the desperation in his voice that got to me. Besides, I didn't have anything else to do. It was kind of nice to be needed, even if I was second choice.

"Do I have to come for supper?" Mrs. Rose was a great cook, but sitting at their dining-room table with Mr. Rose scowling at me over the mashed potatoes was not worth the good food.

"We're done by seven. Don't be late."

Chapter Three

"But I don't want to go to college." Henry sighed.

There I was, sitting on the bottom step of the stairs, only slightly visible to both Henry and his dad, but in clear earshot of the entire conversation. Maybe Henry figured his father would be more agreeable if there was company around, but I didn't think it was working. In fact, I was surprised that Henry thought my presence would influence his father at all. Billy definitely would have been a better choice. Mr. Rose did not like me. I was not Eldred Rose's image of a good role model. He wouldn't even call me PJ, just Peter, which was a sure indication that he hated me.

"Of course you want to go to college," Mr. Rose snapped. "You can't get anywhere in today's world without a college education."

Henry said his dad talked a lot about having put himself

through college, how he'd grown up on a farm and hated it. How he wanted more out of life. He was always telling Henry that he needed to get serious about school. Mr. Rose was serious about everything, and he didn't think Henry was serious about anything.

"Dad," Henry pleaded. "I'm not asking to quit school, just drop a stupid math course. I don't get it. Formulas, theorems, pi stuff. It makes no sense to me."

"It doesn't have to make sense. You just have to learn it." He paused for a moment, peering over the newspaper. "Mrs. Jordan been telling you to quit school again?"

Huh? Henry hadn't said anything about telling his father that Mrs. Jordan suggested he quit school. It was the day he told her he didn't do essays because they don't make him happy. Mrs. Jordan told Henry that didn't make *her* happy, and when Henry told her that he didn't know teachers were supposed to be happy, we all figured Henry was dead. Instead she shrugged her shoulders, peered at him over her glasses, and said either he'd have to quit school or she'd have to retire. Henry didn't even have to stay after school. If it had been me, I probably would have ended up in detention for the week. Who knows why he told his father.

Henry sighed again. It wasn't going quite the way he had planned.

"Oh, for chrissakes, Dad. You know she didn't really mean it. It was just a joke. I wish I hadn't told you."

The paper dropped to his father's lap. "Watch your language!" He paused. "It wasn't funny," he added. "I'm surprised you don't want to drop English, too."

"You can't drop English, Dad. You know that."

"And I know you can't drop math, either, not if you're living in this house."

The newspaper crinkled in Mr. Rose's lap as he peered at Henry over the metal rim of his glasses. I could see the lecture coming. I leaned forward, resting my chin in my hands, my elbows pressed into the tops of my knees. What I really wanted to do was creep backward up the stairs and play video games on Henry's computer. But I had promised. Henry said I needed to be an objective presence, whatever that was.

"Maybe you won't go to college. I guess that's your choice." There was a slight pause. "But you will graduate from high school . . . with math."

His father went on and on, a boring lecture on how to be successful. Once or twice I was sure Mr. Rose glanced at me, especially when he made a comment about "needing good influences" and not being like some people who end up "going nowhere" in life. I found myself examining my boots. I needed new laces, but since I didn't tie them anyway, I guess it didn't matter. I tried to tune him out, but it was pretty hard. Mr. Rose's voice is loud. When I heard ". . . and that's final," I glanced up. The newspaper was in front of Mr. Rose's face once more, blocking any further eye contact between him and Henry. The discussion was over.

It was hopeless. His father would never give in. Henry glanced over to me with his eyebrows raised. Did he really think I could help? I shrugged my shoulders. I had already made some suggestions. Try your mother, I'd told him earlier. His mother struck me as a pretty easy mark. Henry said that was impossible. His mother never went against his father's decisions.

I don't think Henry was really worried about being forced to go to college. Mr. Rose had put himself through college and expected Henry to do the same. If I knew Henry as well as I thought I did, that was not likely to happen. I guess I should be glad nobody is pressuring me to plan my life away. My mom will be thrilled if I graduate from high school, and who knows what my dad expects.

Henry stood in the middle of the living room, the add/drop paper from the guidance office hanging limply in his left hand. He shook his head slightly and tightened his lips. I was sure he was ready to wad that paper up into a ball, throw it onto the floor, and storm out of the room. That's what I would have done. Besides, I was tired of being the "objective presence." He already had my ultimate advice: skip math class and worry about it later.

But Henry stood his ground, and seconds later I saw his shoulders relax. He had said more than once that a show of temper carried no weight with either his father or his mother. They were immune to tantrums and pouts. "Okay, Dad, I'll make a deal."

The newspaper descended into Mr. Rose's lap. I think he was surprised to find Henry still in the room.

"Deal?" He spoke slowly but firmly. "We don't make deals in this house." He began to lift the newspaper up to eye level once more.

I could not believe my eyes. Henry reached out and slowly pulled the top edge of the newspaper back down, forcing his father to make eye contact with him. I held my breath. My heart started to pound. I figured Henry was dead.

"Really, Dad, I got a great idea."

This time it was Mr. Rose who sighed in exasperation. He let the paper fall slowly into his lap and leaned forward. No ranting, no raving. No clearing of the throat for another lecture. Amazing.

"Okay, Henry, what kind of bargain are we talking about here?"

I was impressed. Henry had his interest. Later, Henry told me he'd done some fast thinking. He had had nothing planned out in his head, but he wasn't willing to give up. He said he needed to keep his options open. That was a big mistake.

"Here's the deal, Dad. Let me drop to an easier math class, and I'll raise my grade in English."

He had used the right bait. This was something his father could relate to. Academics. Grades. Success. But raise his grade in English? What a dork.

"To what?"

Henry was clearly caught off guard. He began shifting his weight back and forth from one foot to the other. I don't think he had prepared himself for a compromise. His bargain was a shot in the dark, a long shot.

"Passing?"

That was hardly going to be enough for Mr. Rose. Sure enough, the newspaper began to rise again, waving him away in dismissal.

"Okay, okay, eighty?"

"Ninety," his father countered, lowering the paper onto his lap.

Henry balled his right hand into a fist and shoved it into his heart. "Dad," he moaned, falling backward in the throes of feigned death. As he fell backward, the newspaper rose quickly once more.

Henry leaped forward. "Eighty-five. I can do eighty-five."

"You can do ninety," Mr. Rose said as he closed the newspaper and folded it in half, placing it on the floor beside his chair. He turned slightly and picked up the coffee cup from the end table beside him. "But I will settle for eighty-five."

Henry's jaw dropped and he stared at his father. I think he even forgot I was there.

"You will?"

"Yes, Henry, I will. That and a ninety in the easier math course. If you can promise me that, I will sign the paper."

Henry looked away from his father and began studying the floor. An uncomfortable silence filled the room.

"That's it, Henry. Take it or leave it."

His father rose from the chair, coffee cup in hand, heading toward the kitchen. Henry had to decide. It was clearly a last-chance proposition, and he was the one who had proposed a deal. He was trapped. *No, No, No!* I wanted to holler out. *Don't cave in to the enemy!*

Henry held the paper out to his father.

"Sign here."

Mr. Rose reached into his shirt pocket and whipped out a pen, signed the paper as he held it against Henry's back, and exited toward the kitchen without another word.

Henry trudged slowly toward me, scowling.

"I've been had."

"Yup." I was no consolation.

"I guess I got myself into this," he said as he stepped around me and headed upstairs.

"Yup," I agreed. "You want me to go home now?"

"Not yet," he moaned. "My misery needs company."

He continued up the stairs, and I followed. It didn't matter much to me. I had nothing to go home for.

Chapter Four

Upstairs in his bedroom, Henry threw himself facedown on his bed, instantly rolled over onto his back, and began rocking from side to side as he covered his face with his hands. I thought he was being a little dramatic.

"I'm doomed, PJ," he moaned.

"What's the big deal here, Henry? You change math courses and then quit worrying. You think your father's going to remember this deal?"

He sat up and threw his hands into the air, flinging a pillow across the room and onto the floor. A pretty nice floor, too, I might add. The Roses have money and Henry's room has big, fat carpeting over the whole floor. The pillow made no sound as it fell, adding to the quiet drama of the moment. He swung his legs slowly over the side of the bed and sat there staring at me. It was as though I had said something incredibly stupid.

"You don't get it," he said quietly. "My father does not make bargains, does not compromise. Were you listening? There were no other conditions, no 'what if I don't do it?' I agreed to this. He signed my paper. I'm doomed."

Henry's sincerity was amazing. I don't think my mother even knew what courses I was taking. And my father? My father's life was a series of bad bargains, broken promises, and deals that he never lived up to.

"I agreed to this," he repeated as though I hadn't heard him. "I have to make those grades. I should have stayed in Course II and toughed it out. An eighty-five in English and a ninety in Intro to Course II? This sucks."

"Can you do it?"

"Of course I can do it," he snapped back at me, sounding way too much like his father. "But not without doing my work." He threw himself back onto the pillowless bed in defeat and moaned. "What was I thinking?"

It seemed like Mr. Rose had gotten the better deal here. Somehow Henry had been lured into his father's value system.

"Well, I know I wouldn't do it."

"You don't have Eldred Henry Rose for a father."

It was true. I didn't. Henry's father was demanding and boring. But at least he knew his son existed. Mine was a parental disaster.

Suddenly Henry sprang from the bed. He grabbed his backpack off his desk and began rummaging through it.

"You gotta help me, PJ. We've got an essay due tomorrow."

"We do?"

"If I'm gonna pull this off, I might just as well get started," he explained, pulling one of Mrs. Jordan's famous yellow assignment sheets out of his pack. Mrs. Jordan was color-coded: blue for vocabulary, yellow for essays, green for worksheets. Did she think we were still in elementary school?

"*You* have an essay due, Henry. I don't do essays, remember?" The new Henry was already a disaster. "I'm going home," I announced as I hopped off his dresser, where I had been perched.

"Nooo," Henry wailed. He sounded pathetic. "Moral support, PJ. You promised."

"You just sold your morals, Henry, right back to your father."

"Please," he begged. He was on his knees in front of me. I guess he was trying to be funny. Frankly, he *was* pathetic.

"Okay, okay. I'll stay. But I am not helping you write some stupid-ass essay." I plunked down at Henry's desk and opened the games folder on his computer. "This is as supportive as I can be."

"Look at it this way," he said, poking me in the back. "Mrs. Jordan will be surprised, maybe even shocked. She's always saying I'm a good enough reason to retire. Maybe this will do it."

I don't think driving Mrs. Jordan out of her job was a particular goal of Henry's. Actually, I think he kind of liked her. At least he wasn't afraid of her like lots of her students. Probably because he had so much practice dealing with his father.

By ten o'clock, Henry's essay was still not finished. He had started it a dozen times. Every time he reread his opening paragraph, it sounded lame or just plain stupid. Mrs. Jordan hadn't seen much of his writing, he said, and so it needed to be good. It was six weeks into the school year and he'd only done a couple writing assignments. I hadn't done any.

"I've got to impress her. It's got to be good," he said as he crumpled up another piece of paper with two sentences written on it. I thought he was working pretty hard at not doing it.

"If you're gonna do it, just do it, Henry. It doesn't have to be good. It just has to be done."

"Did you hear my father, PJ? Eighty-five in English. It can't be *just* done. It has to be good."

The assignment should not have been a difficult one for him: it was about making decisions in life. Well, he had just made a bad decision as far as I could see, but he was trying to write what he thought Mrs. Jordan would want to hear, and it sounded phony. She was not stupid; she would see right through him.

"This is not working. I'm doomed. I might just as well admit defeat."

"So rip up the damn add/drop sheet and go on with life." I was tired of the drama.

"I can't. Not now." His voice got low and serious. "My father and I will probably never see eye to eye on much, but I can't bear the thought of him thinking I'm a total failure, PJ. I made a deal."

I had never seen Henry this sincere. He meant it. It was also embarrassing. Nobody had ever poured their heart out to me. Not even Heather. I clicked out of the computer game and gave him my full attention. PJ was coming to the rescue.

"Okay, Henry. First of all, you have to get Mrs. Jordan on your side. Tell her changing won't be easy for you, but convince her that you are really going to try."

"Fat chance."

I threw my hands up in frustration. "Look, you want my advice. This is it. Take it or leave it."

"You think I ought to go see her? Ask for an extension?"

"Well, that might work." Secretly, I figured he was doomed. Mrs. Jordan didn't take late work. And the thought of going to see her, before school, before class? Staying after school because she said you had to was one thing, but going to see her on purpose? I wouldn't do that.

"You wanta go see her?"

Henry's gloom turned into an instant grin.

"You have got to be kidding," he laughed. "On the other hand . . ." The grin grew wider. "I could go see her and tell her I'm having a writing breakdown, that the emotional struggle between me and my computer is more than I can handle."

"You idiot," I snapped as I threw a CD case at him.

Henry was the class clown. It was easy for him to make smart remarks in class, smirk, and be flip about anything in front of his classmates, which, actually, was pretty amazing, considering his genes.

"You're right"—he sighed, the grin gone—"that's probably not a good idea."

"Then there's only one way."

"There is?"

"Yup. Write her a letter."

"A letter?"

"Explain the situation. Ask for an extension."

"A letter."

"Yeah. Just turn it in when she collects the essays. Trust me. It's your best chance at this point."

I didn't know whether or not it was Henry's best chance, but I was pretty tired of all the attention on schoolwork. I turned back to the computer.

"Letter. Yeah, a letter. Good idea. I'll write her a letter."

"Quit yapping and write the damn letter, Henry."

Henry grabbed a fresh sheet of paper and plunked himself back down on his bed. Fifteen minutes later, he waved the finished product in front of my eyes.

"You want to read it?"

One click and I was out of the game. I took a deep breath, heaved up my shoulders, and let them drop again in exaggerated exasperation. I offered my right hand, palm up.

"Give it here," I demanded.

Henry handed over the letter, and I read through it quickly.

Dear Mrs. Jordan:

I know you will probably not believe me, but I really tried to do the essay tonight and I just couldn't. Maybe I have nothing to say or maybe I waited too late, but it just isn't happening. The topic is not a difficult one. I know that. We all make decisions every day. Some of them are good ones and some are not so good and probably some are really lousy ones. And maybe this is not a good decision, my trying to explain why

I didn't do my homework, but the fact that I am even trying to do my essay is, frankly, the result of having made a really poor decision.

You see, I made a deal with my father tonight and that, in itself, was probably my first mistake. One should never make deals with parents, especially my father. Parents have all the control. A decision which involves trying to control that control definitely shows poor decision-making skills on anyone's part.

My second mistake was not backing out when I had the chance. I guess we all probably make some poor decisions in our lives and obviously need to recognize when indeed they are poor ones. The best course of action would have been to have stopped the deal before it was completed, acknowledge it was not in my best interest, and go from there. But I didn't. And now I am chained to a course of action that is bound to infringe upon my lifestyle at the very least or destroy my father's faith in me at the very worst if I should not follow through.

Nonetheless, I am imploring you to show some mercy and allow me an opportunity for an extension. I know that my request is far beyond the bounds of your expectations for your students, but we all must make difficult decisions in our lives and I am sure teachers must do so, too. If you decide to grant me this extension, I shall not fail you. I also promise not to smirk in class anymore.

Your student,
Henry Rose

I handed the paper back to Henry slowly, trying to determine my best course of action. Do I keep him as a partner in procrastination, a fellow miserable student, a best friend . . . at least when Billy wasn't available? Or do I encourage him to follow this new path, one requiring way too much energy. I chose truth.

"It'll work. Can I go home now?"

Chapter Five

The bell had rung, and there I was, late to class again. Life sure would be easier if I didn't have English first period. Maybe I could change my schedule. Take social studies or art first period. Mr. Gridley and Mrs. Hempstead don't care whether you come late to class or not. Their doors aren't closed and locked at the bell.

I stood outside the door, my back pressed against the cold, hard metal of a locker. I hate making decisions. If I skipped, I could count on detention for a day or two. If I knocked at the door, Mrs. Jordan would ask for my pass. I didn't have one and wasn't likely to get one from anyone either. I'd already used up my "seek out the new teachers who didn't know any better" list. If I hung out in the hall much longer, I was going to have to deal with the monitor as she made her rounds.

"Where're you supposed to be, PJ?"

Too late. It was Mrs. White. Hall monitor with an attitude. Just what I needed. She'd snuck up the hall from the library and I hadn't even seen her coming, maybe because I was trying to peek in the window to the classroom to see if Mrs. Jordan had really started class. She had.

"English," I replied honestly, pointing slightly toward Room 118.

Her eyebrows scrunched together quickly. For a brief moment, I thought maybe I could get her to give me a pass. No such luck.

"Well, then I suggest you get in there. You're in trouble already. No point in making it worse."

Great. Tell me something I don't know.

And then she made things worse. She drew up her big paw of a hand and rapped on the door. Three times. So loud that the noise echoed down the hall. What the hell did she think she was doing?

The door opened and Mrs. Jordan stood there. She didn't say a word. She just looked at us. First at Mrs. White and then at me. I could see past her into the classroom. Everybody was watching us. Dead silence.

"PJ's late," Mrs. White announced loudly. Brilliant observation.

"I see that, Mrs. White. Thank you for bringing him to class."

Mrs. Jordan nodded for me to enter and then closed the door behind me without another word to the hall Nazi.

"Take your seat, PJ, and please stay after class for a moment."

Here we go. In trouble for being four seconds late to class. Let's see. That ought to be worth two weeks of after-school detention. No, maybe a month. Yeah, that's probably more like it.

"PJ?"

"Huh?"

"I asked you if you had your homework."

"What homework?" I had brought my book to class. I thought that was pretty good. In fact, going to my locker to get my book was what made me late to begin with. Of course if I had come to class without my book, she would have told me to go get it, and I still would have been late. You can't win, can you?

Wrong answer. She gave me one of her icy stares, the kind that looks like she's thinking too hard. But she didn't say anything more to me. In fact, she ignored me for the rest of the period. That worked for me.

When the bell rang at the end of class, I did not forget that Mrs. Jordan had asked me to stay after. But I hoped *she* had. I grabbed my book and slid into the line of students filing out through the door. It didn't work.

"PJ? I asked you to stay, please."

She was still sitting on her stool in the front of the classroom where she had been at the end of the period. I stepped out of the line and turned toward her slightly, bracing myself for the lecture.

"I got gym."

"This won't take long. If necessary, I'll write you a pass," she said as she slid off her stool and moved past me to close the door. I was expecting the lecture-to-end-all-lectures.

"First of all, the worksheets you did after school yesterday were less than satisfactory. I would have you stay after school today, but I have a meeting. So, when you stay tomorrow, we will work on them together. And since you did not have your essay ready for today, I will expect you to work on that as well."

"Yeah, okay." I didn't think she knew I had a soccer game after school tomorrow. It didn't matter; she wouldn't have cared.

"Also, PJ, I need to ask you about something."

I had been examining my boots pretty thoroughly, but the change in her voice made me look up. She didn't look angry.

"Huh?"

"I'm missing something, and I thought maybe it was with the materials I gave you yesterday afternoon."

I stared at her. What was she was talking about?

"The homework papers, PJ? The ones I gave you last night?"

"Oh, yeah, those papers. Yeah, I have them. I just don't have them all done yet." Done? They were probably on the floor in my room where I had dumped stuff out of my backpack before going over to Henry's. I had totally forgotten about them. Homework was not high on my list of priorities.

"Well, I am missing an important notebook, and I was hoping that it was with the materials I had given you."

A notebook? How important could a notebook be?

"I didn't see anything."

"Are you sure, PJ? It is pretty important to me. It's blue. About so big."

She framed the size of a sheet of paper with her hands and then lifted the thumb and index finger of her right hand to indicate something about a half-inch thick. I didn't think the measurements were all that necessary, especially since I had just told her I hadn't seen it.

"I didn't see anything," I insisted.

"Oh." She sounded disappointed, not angry. "I was sure it must have been with those materials."

"I gotta go, Mrs. Jordan." Part of me wanted to ask her for that pass she had offered, but mostly I wanted out of there.

"Okay, PJ, but if you see this notebook—"

"I told you I don't have it," I snapped.

I guess I shouldn't have cut her off like that. I didn't mean to. It just happened. She gave me another one of those Mrs. Jordan glares and nodded.

"You better go, then, or you'll be late to your next class."

There was no offer of a pass.

Chapter Six

By 8:54 my day had already been ruined, and it only got worse.
You know how it works. Nothing goes right. I was late to gym and
had to run endless laps while everyone else hung around the tennis courts, the preps posing with their rackets while half a dozen
kids bounced tennis balls back and forth with their hands. It was
pretty warm for October, and the gym teachers were making use
of every spare ray of sunshine. It just made me tired. I fell asleep
in social studies, and science was no fun without Henry to fool
around with. He'd left early for a dentist appointment. Soccer
practice was pretty normal, I guess. Brian Carson stomped around
acting important, and Coach Lockwood yelled more than ever.
The only good thing about the day was that we got out of practice
early so we could rest up for the big game against Preston. Even
that wasn't so good, though, since my mom was working late at

the hospital, and that meant Frank and I would be alone together for way too long.

Frank's my stepdad. We get along okay as long as we don't have too much to do with each other. I never knew how he and my mother met. I didn't care. One day, he was just there, complete with clothes and tools. That was a couple months before my parents' divorce was final, which wasn't a big deal, since my dad hadn't lived with us for over a year. Two months after the divorce, Frank and my mom got married. Nobody ever asked me what I thought. The only thing my mom said to me about Frank before they got married was that I could call him Frank, that he wasn't going to try to be my dad. That was pretty funny, since even my dad hadn't ever tried to be much of a dad.

When I got home from school, Frank was working on his truck. He was always working on his truck. Sometimes he had a real job. Most of the time he didn't. But with his head stuck under the raised hood, at least I didn't have to have a conversation with him. I headed into the house, dropped my backpack at the foot of the stairs, and plunked down in front of the TV.

Several music videos later I heard the sound of water running in the kitchen, and within seconds the smell of cigarette smoke filled the air. Suddenly I was thirsty, and I headed into the kitchen for a soda.

"Saw you come home. Kinda early, huh?" He was glancing through the classified ad section of the paper.

"Game tomorrow," I offered, not that it mattered. I'm not sure Frank even knew what sport I played. Neither he nor my mom ever came to my games. Frank isn't much of a sports person, except for stuff like NASCAR and WWE.

"Oh, yeah. Your dad called this morning," Frank drawled as I was reaching into the refrigerator. "The message is still on the machine."

"Thanks, Frank," I grumbled. "I don't suppose you could have told me this earlier." I had been home at least an hour.

"Didn't think of it."

I wanted to tell him he didn't think much at all, but we didn't need a fight. We'd been getting along pretty well lately, at least for us. I flung the refrigerator door shut and headed into the living room to check the answering machine.

"Wednesday, nine forty-eight A.M."

Nine forty-eight? He knew I'd be in school.

"Hey there, PJ. Look, about this weekend. Something's come up, and we just aren't going to be able to go. Sorry. Talk to you later."

"End of messages."

Camping this weekend had not exactly been my activity of choice, but, hell, why not? I'd borrowed a sleeping bag and a backpack big enough for an overnight hike from Billy. The plan was to go to Lake Placid Saturday morning and then hike up to Marcy Dam, where we would camp in a lean-to for the night. Sunday morning we would climb Marcy, return to camp, pick up our gear, and head home. A lot of work for a little adventure, but my dad was great at coming up with big ideas that didn't make sense. It was mid-October. Probably too late for stupid hikers and campers to be wandering around the Adirondacks anyway. But I was still pissed.

"Thanks, Dad. Thanks a lot," I muttered.

"Plans fell though again, huh?" Frank was leaning against the doorway which separated the kitchen from the living room, taking deep drags from his cigarette.

"None of your business, Frank."

"Hey there, PJ. No need to jump down my throat."

I stormed past him into the kitchen and grabbed my jacket off the hook.

"Where ya goin'?"

"Out," I snapped as I stormed out the back door and let it slam behind me. I didn't care what Frank thought. He wasn't my father. After all, he really didn't care what I did. Nobody did. It was the second time this month my dad had called to say he wouldn't be picking me up. I wasn't surprised. I'm supposed to see him every other weekend, but it doesn't usually work out that way. More like every other month . . . or two.

I didn't know where I was headed, just away from home. With each step, I grew more and more angry. It was stupid. My dad was just being my dad, and Frank was just being Frank.

I moved like a man on a mission, heading toward the center of town. The problem was I had no mission, no place to go. It was too close to supper time to drop in on Billy or Henry. Besides, I never just drop in on them. I always wait to be asked. I'm not sure why. They drop in on each other all the time. But then, they're best friends.

Speaking of supper, I was hungry. Usually it's every man for himself at my house, which means Frank and I eat lots of peanut butter, but sometimes we eat when my mom gets home from work, if it isn't too late. My stomach said food. Now.

There are only two places in Bradford for food. The pizza place was the best bet, since only people who are over thirty go to Kate's

Diner. It didn't matter anyway. I was broke. It's hard calling your own shots when you're poor and have no place to go. That is a major problem. I never have any money.

My dad is supposed to pay child support, but my mom doesn't let me forget that he never has, not a dime. Whenever I need money for anything, she reminds me that it's really my father's responsibility, that if my father would meet his obligations, then she could meet hers. So sometimes it's easier to dip into the jar of change she keeps in the back of the kitchen cupboard. She never seems to notice anything's missing, and Frank probably doesn't even know it's there. Sometimes I feel guilty. Mostly I don't.

I wished I'd grabbed a handful of change before I left the house, but I'd been too annoyed to even think of it. Besides, that would have been impossible with Frank standing in the kitchen. The last thing I need is for Frank to discover an easy source of ready cash, even if it is mostly nickels and dimes.

Hungry and broke. It was enough to piss anyone off.

A screech of brakes and an angry horn caught me off guard as a black Jeep Wrangler stopped abruptly at the intersection of East Main and Chapel Street, where I had just stepped off the curb.

"For chrissakes, Barnes. You got eyes?" Brian Carson yelled out his window.

"Learn to drive," I shouted back as I flipped him off and stalked across the street in front of him. Now he could be pissed off, too. Which wasn't the smartest thing to do. I was already his target. Only I would do something this dumb.

"Well, you never will," he yelled after me. "You won't live that long if you keep actin' like an idiot."

Idiot? He should talk. He was just an idiot with wheels. Pretty good wheels, I had to admit. Must be nice to get a new Jeep Wrangler for your birthday, something I would never know about.

Being poor sucks. Hungry and broke and scorned by the Brian Carsons of the world, who always seem to get what they want. Even Heather used to tease me about how loving a rich man would be a lot easier than loving a poor one. I wonder if she thinks Nick the Nerd is the next Bill Gates.

I had found my mission. What I needed was a job.

An hour later, I was an employee at Midtown Market. Well, I was going to be as soon as I got my working papers. Stocking shelves for ten hours a week at minimum wage was not going to make me rich, but it was a start. I didn't need my dad. I didn't need Heather. Life was good. I was ready to go home.

Chapter Seven

"I don't know, PJ. It doesn't seem like you've thought this out very well. What about school?"

I couldn't believe my ears! She should've been glad, even happy for me. There we were, sitting around the table eating hot dogs and Tater Tots and missing the point that I had done something pretty neat.

"For chrissakes, you're always telling me how we have no money. You oughta be glad I got a job."

"I had a job when I was fifteen," Frank offered. My mother ignored him. So did I. He was not the ideal role model. I'm sure even my mother knew that.

"You have school. How are you going to take on a job?" She reached for the salt. "Pass the ketchup, please, Frank."

"I'm doin' okay." An absolute lie. It was only six weeks into the school year, and I was probably failing everything. But I was always failing everything in the fall, and I always squeaked by at the end of the year.

"I got time," I continued. "What else have I got to do? It's not like there's a ton of stuff to sit around home for."

"You passing everything?" She was dolloping ketchup onto her plate, ready for dipping each lump of browned potato mass.

"Sure." Another lie. She asked about school and homework once in a while, but she never followed up on anything, never came to school unless she had to. Why wouldn't she stop eating and pay attention? This was important. I needed her permission. She had to sign the papers.

"What about football?"

"Soccer."

"Huh?"

"I play soccer, Mom."

"Right. Well, what about it? Are you just going to quit?"

"Maybe. I haven't figured that out yet. The season's over pretty soon anyway. Besides, isn't a job more important than some dumb sport?"

"I don't know. What would your father think about this? Have you asked him yet?"

My father? Of course I hadn't asked my father. Why would I? The bastard can't be bothered with me most of the time. Why would he care whether or not I had a job? In fact, he would probably be thrilled. It would justify not sending any money.

"Well?" my mother pressed. "Did you call and ask his permission?"

The blood surged upward through my body as my palms

pushed down hard against the edge of the table. The next thing I knew my chair had fallen backward onto the floor, and I was leaning against the table.

"No! I did not call my father," I yelled. "What the hell does he care?"

"You don't need to swear at me, PJ."

Frank glanced up slightly, but then he shrugged his shoulders and returned to his meal, sorting through his food, one hand holding his fork, the other his *Motor Trend* magazine. He was generally willing to let my mother and me fight our own battles.

"You get his permission, and I'll sign," she added as she lifted her cup of coffee to her lips, blew gently over the edge, and took a sip. Sometimes she was way too calm when we fought. It drove me crazy.

This was stupid. My father would give permission. I knew that. But the papers needed only one signature. And my mother knew my father would give permission. He didn't care enough not to. So what was the point? It was like she was playing some game, making a chess move, and I was the pawn about to be sacrificed. Well, I was not about to be used.

"Frank?" New strategy. "How about if you sign them?"

"Huh?" He quit chewing for a moment and looked up from his magazine. "Sign what?"

"Oh, for chrissakes." I threw my hands in the air in defeat. Here I was, maybe taking the most important step in my life, and no one would take me seriously. "Look, Mom, if I call Dad and get his permission, will you sign the papers?"

"You get his permission and prove to me you are passing everything." Her fork stabbed another Tater Tot. "Then I will sign your working papers."

Doomed.

"Never mind. It was a lousy idea anyway."

I left them munching on Oreos and headed upstairs, grabbing my backpack from the bottom step and hurling it up the stairs ahead of me. Why did everyone have to make life so damn complicated? I stomped up the stairs and slammed my bedroom door behind me, but with the TV in the kitchen already blaring, it was a pointless act of defiance.

So now what? Homework? Yeah, right. Did my mother really think I would become Super Student overnight? On the other hand, my bedroom was hardly the ideal refuge, not like Henry's room. No television, no computer, no video games, no phone. I didn't even have a CD player, much less an iPod.

I had decided to just pack it all up and go to bed, even though the hot dogs and Tater Tots were still settling in my stomach, when I remembered that I had Henry's copy of *Rolling Stone* in my backpack. I dug into the pack, Academy Broadway, basic green and cheap, straight from Wal-Mart. No magazine. It had to be there. I had just borrowed it a couple days ago. Nope, no magazine. Just a couple movies I'd borrowed from Henry.

That was it. Before I went over to Henry's the night before, I had dumped everything on the floor, filling my pack with the videos I needed to return to him. Yep, there on the floor was the stuff I had crammed into it after school yesterday in Mrs. Jordan's room. If I hadn't already been late to practice, I'd have ditched it all in my locker.

I picked up the pile and threw it on my unmade bed. What a mess. Most of it was the stuff from Mrs. Jordan, including a copy of *A Midsummer Night's Dream*, which isn't a bad story if you are into people running around in the woods taking drugs and falling in love with jackasses . . . which, when you think about it, happens around here quite a lot. Maybe Shakespeare knew what he was talking about. It was the second copy Mrs. Jordan had given me this year. I guess she figured I'd lost the first one. I hadn't. It was somewhere in my locker.

The copy of *Rolling Stone* was nowhere to be seen. This was crazy. It had to be there somewhere. I knew I hadn't looked at it since Henry gave it to me. So I spread out all the stuff on the bed: two essay assignments, three vocabulary worksheets, a stack of handouts and worksheets on the Elizabethan period, and . . . a notebook, the kind we used to have in middle school. We had to write at least five sentences in it every day. We could write on anything: friends, school, family, life, death, sports, food. The list was endless. The teacher guaranteed our right to freedom of speech. No one would check on us. No one would put a grade on it. By the end of the year, mine was as blank as it was on the first day. No one noticed. On the last day of class, we were told to take it home and keep it, that twenty years from now we would enjoy reading it. On my way out of class, I dumped mine in the recycling box, which eased my guilt somewhat about the waste of paper.

So what was Mrs. Jordan thinking? Was this for me now? Had she somehow discovered my seventh-grade deceit? Was I doomed to make up everything I had not done in every English class I had ever taken? I was just about to toss the notebook, the *blue* notebook, into the wastebasket (I was no longer environmentally conscientious) when the writing in the upper right-hand corner of the cover flashed like a neon sign . . . *Clarice Jordan*.

Clarice Jordan?

Holy shit! I dropped it on the bed instantly. Just seeing the name sent chills up my spine. I'd never thought about Mrs. Jordan having a name—that is, a first name.

I was afraid to open it up, as afraid as I would be if I were knocking on the door of her home, asking her to buy magazines for the sophomore class or cheese for the booster club, not that I would ever be caught dead doing either of those things. Mrs. Jordan was scary enough in her classroom. But here she was in my bedroom, first name and all, and it did not seem right.

Clarice Jordan? If you knew Mrs. Jordan, you'd have to agree that she does not seem like a Clarice. She's pretty old. Fifty? Sixty? Seems like a Clarice should be young, maybe with long, blond hair and blue eyes, and kind of small. Sort of like Heather. She could be a Clarice. Mrs. Jordan has mostly gray hair, kind of short and curly, and who knows what color her eyes are. I don't look at teachers that much. I guess she's not all that tall, but she seems so when she's standing up there in the front of the classroom.

Suddenly there was a sharp rap on my door.

"PJ? You doing your homework?"

My heart stopped. The door opened slightly. As my mother's sweatshirted arm pushed the door open farther, I slid the notebook under my backpack. I don't know why. I'd done nothing wrong. I sat on the edge of the bed as she stepped into the room.

"What are you doing?"

"Nothin'." I leaned to the right slightly, resting my elbow on top of my backpack.

"You look guilty, PJ. I know guilt when I see it." If we hadn't fought at supper, I would've thought she was teasing me. But her voice was cranky. She was right. I felt guilty. I should have shown her the notebook right then, should have told her I didn't know how I got it. Except I did. When Mrs. Jordan gave me that stuff the day before, she must have picked up her notebook, too. So why not just say so?

"I'm not doin' anything," I grumbled.

"That's what I came to check on. Look, maybe getting a job will work, but you have to do okay in school." She leaned against the door frame, looking as though she were settling in for a night of supervising the criminal. "You must have homework. Have you finished it yet?"

"Finished? I just got up here," I blurted out. It was true. How could I possibly have had time to have finished anything? That's the trouble with parents, isn't it? They give you an order and expect it to be done before you have time to figure out what it is they want you to do.

Then again, maybe she was weakening. Maybe she was ready to give in, ready to sign my working papers. Maybe I should have told her yes, my homework was finished. She stood in the doorway, right shoulder leaning against the door frame, her arms folded across her chest with the fingers of her right hand tapping her left elbow, her lips pressed firmly together, and her forehead scrunched up so that her eyebrows almost touched each other above her nose. She did not look particularly weak.

"So? Where's the homework?"

I lifted some papers beside me and dropped them once more onto the bed. I rolled my eyes and heaved a huge sigh.

"So much?" She shook her head from side to side. "So far behind already?"

I shrugged my shoulders. What good was an explanation. There was no explanation.

"When it's done, we'll talk about the job." She stepped backward into the hall and pulled the door closed.

Safe.

I waited until I was sure she was not going to fling open the door and pounce, eager to catch me in the act of shirking my responsibilities. I sat on the edge of the bed, my hands gripping the sheet, for what seemed like forever. At least forty-five seconds passed before I reached under the backpack, my eyes fixed on the closed door, and pulled out the blue notebook. It really didn't look like anything special, just one of those plain light blue notebooks that teachers really did give us in middle school. My heart was pounding as I opened the front cover. There on the inside cover, written very neatly, it said:

Clarice Jordan

Thoughts and Observations

I flipped through the first few pages. Some of the writing was in blue or black ink, a few sections were in pencil. Some pages had a date at the top. Some did not.

The dog days of summer end soon, perhaps all too soon. Am I so reluctant to begin the new school year? Am I too eager to hold on to the laziness of August mornings . . .

Bo-o-o-r-r-ring. It better get better than this.

Chapter Eight

"Go, Go, Go, Go, Go!"

Coach Lockwood's low roar followed us down the field. I could tell he was shouting commands as he hustled down the sideline, but the rush of wind in my ears drowned them out. It didn't matter. Coach yelled all the time we were on the field. Even when he wasn't yelling at us, he was still yelling. No one took the game of soccer as seriously as Loudmouth Lockwood did. It was his life, and I guess he figured it was everyone else's.

Unfortunately for Coach, soccer wasn't our whole life. Except for maybe Brian Carson, who wanted to play soccer at college. Brian was pissed at us most of the time, felt we were ruining his chances at a scholarship because no scout would come looking for college material on a team whose record was 0 and 7. He was good, but he refused to admit that anyone else was. To him, being captain meant he could yell at us no matter what we did, and we had learned we could tune him out almost as easily as we did Coach.

"Oh, for chrissakes, Jackson."

I heard Coach clearly that time, and I was sure Billy had, too. Letting the opponent steal the pass—well, at least what appeared to be a pass—was sport sin. Forget that our captain often drove the ball down the field, ignoring his teammates and getting so out of control that, just before he went sprawling over his own feet, he would jab one last time at the ball, an attempted pass to no one in particular. It was always intercepted. Most of us on the team called it stupidity. Coach called it hustle. And whoever was closest to Brian got the blame.

"Thanks a lot, Jackson," Brian grumbled as he slid behind Billy to move back into position. Brian's position was center forward, but it didn't really matter. He played whatever position he wanted, and then grumbled that he had to do everyone else's job. We all wished that a college scout would come to see one of our games. He could see Brian in action. He could see what an asshole he was.

The horn blew as subs came onto the field, and I heard Morgan Jones bellow out Billy's name just as Kevin Andrews tapped me from behind. I hustled to the sideline, then dropped my pace instantly, moving slowly toward the bench as Billy caught up with me. Here we were, once more, subbed out before the first quarter was over. Billy plunked down onto the bench next to Henry. I plopped down beside Billy. It didn't matter much to me. I wasn't very good. But Billy was. In fact, he was probably one of the better players, but he was a sophomore and the unwritten rule was that seniors and juniors got more playing time.

Billy and I couldn't complain too much. Henry only got to play if other players were injured. I was impressed that he stayed with the team. Most of us would have quit long before this. Coach told us that he tried to put every player in every game, and that when some guys improved their skills, they would get more playing time. Those of us who kept the bench warm most of the time kept trying to figure how we would get better if we were never allowed to play.

"So much for the hair, huh?" Henry sounded truly forlorn.

"Well, I guess we shouldn't expect miracles," Billy commiserated.

The words I'd read last night in Mrs. Jordan's journal flashed like a neon sign in my head: Billy Jackson and his teammates must think their blond—almost orange—hair means something. Power? Attention from the coach? Barry may think losing 5-0 instead of 8-0 is an improvement for his team, but I'm not sure hair is the answer.

"I don't want miracles. I just want to play," Henry sighed. He jabbed Billy in the ribs with his elbow. "I guess that would be a miracle," he chuckled.

"Don't give up hope," I urged. "The game has just started."

But right then, the Preston team scored a goal, and as a cheer rose up in the bleachers across the field, Billy and Henry and I sighed in unison. Our playing time was probably over for this game.

"I shouldn't have done it," Henry remarked vacantly, staring straight at the field, even though the play had moved to the other end.

"Done what?" Billy asked.

"Bleached my hair. Monica hates it. She wants me to dye it brown."

Mrs. Jordan would probably agree.

"You gonna do it?" Billy asked.

I knew Billy was not too thrilled with his own look. The novelty had worn off quickly, and it had caused too much trouble with his parents. Maybe if Henry rebelled against the pro look, he would, too. Me? I really didn't care. I even thought about keeping it just to annoy Heather, which was pretty stupid because I apparently could drop dead for all she cared.

"She says it better be back to normal by the junior prom or we're through."

"Think she means it?" Billy's voice expressed the worry we both felt for Henry.

Henry glanced over his shoulder, scanning the bleachers behind us. Monica Watson, Tracy Johnston, and Amanda Cummings sat side by side in the second row. In unison, they lifted their right hands from their laps in a little wave. I assumed it was all for Henry, who returned the waves with a nod and then turned his head back toward us and raised his eyebrows. The look on his face said it all.

"Monica? You really wonder whether or not Monica means it?"

Billy paused for a moment and then shook his head slowly from side to side. He gave a sigh that must have emptied his lungs and then dropped his head so that his chin pressed into the lower part of his neck. "You're doomed."

"Yep," I added, "you are definitely doomed."

Monica Watson went through boyfriends like bathroom paper cups, taking small drinks and then crushing them with one hand before dropping them lightly into the wastebasket. And yet each of them found himself grateful for her attention, groveling at her feet, hoping against hope that, in him, she had found her true love. Henry had felt particularly special when Monica began hanging out near his locker. He's a sophomore, she's a junior. He had never had a date; Monica had probably been dating since kindergarten. For a week, we all wondered if her interest was real or if she was using him to make someone jealous. Henry didn't care. His popularity had zoomed to uncharted heights in that one week, and had Monica dumped him, he still would have been happy for the rest of his life, or at least the rest of sophomore year. But she didn't. In fact, they had been dating for almost a month, and no one was more surprised than Henry and Monica. The rest of us were waiting for the bomb to fall.

"I know. I know."

Henry moaned so pathetically that Billy put his arm around his friend's shoulder, eager to comfort the sick and the wounded.

"Barnes, Jackson, Rose, on your feet. Let's go."

Lockwood's barking startled us back to the game. We jumped forward to the sideline, only to notice three players limping off the field. While wallowing in our own misery, we had stopped watching the game and had failed to see the collision of three of our own teammates. So much for hair and team spirit.

"Rose, in for Andrews; Jackson, in for Kelsey; Barnes for Pettrick. Let's see some hustle, and for cryin' out loud, Rose, don't screw up."

Ouch! I saw the wave of anger flood over Billy. Attacking Henry was like beating up on a member of Billy's own family. He doesn't anger easily, but when he does, his jaw clenches, his arms drop straight to his sides, and his shoulders rise about four inches. It's pretty interesting, if you're not on the other end of his wrath.

"Lousy Loudmouth," I heard him mutter as he passed in front of me. Knowing Billy, I would not have been surprised if he had walked off the field and thrown his jersey onto the ground in front of Coach, willing to die for the cause of human decency. On the other hand, I was feeling a little guilty, grateful that I was not the target of scorn. I glanced quickly toward Henry. No anger. No embarrassment. I wasn't surprised. Henry Rose is a man of forgiveness. He never shows signs of resentment, never indicates outwardly that he ever feels slighted or abused. He is also used to it. Whatever did Monica see in him?

"Let's go. Let's go. Let's see some hustle out there. C'mon, ladies, move it, move it, move it!"

Ladies? Ladies? That did it. Lockwood wanted hustle? He was going to get it. Billy was pissed off, and now so was I. Billy was defending his friend's dignity; I was ready to defend my manhood. We both hurried into position.

Brian Carson had placed himself in prime position to receive the throw-in, bouncing back and forth, shouting at Ryan Marlow to notice him, but Billy was edging forward, about to make his move. As the throw-in bounced awkwardly past Brian's left leg, Billy slid around behind him and brought the ball under control with his right foot. Brian, caught off guard, stopped on the field and threw his hands into the air.

"Geesh, Carson, let's go. Move it." Coach's voice came through loud and clear. And the scolding of his star player escaped no one, especially not Brian.

Billy had already taken off down the field, two opponents pressing hard on his heels to push him out of control. My heart was pounding as I tried to keep up. Billy's a pretty strong runner, but I suspected he was moving mostly on anger. And energy from anger was not going to last. I was right. With two bodies pressing close behind him, he tried to pull back and check his position before he totally lost his momentum. But it was too late. A black shoe shot quickly toward the ball and moved it easily out of bounds.

"I got it. I got it," Henry shouted. He hopped over the line and the referee tossed the ball to him. In the few seconds it took for Henry to set himself up and look for an opening, Brian was at Billy's side.

"If you can't take it all the way, Jackson, you better let someone who can."

I knew the snide tone was nothing more than Brian covering up for his own fumbling minutes earlier, but I was tired of everybody else being the scapegoat. Billy and I made eye contact. His eyes were blazing with anger and his face was flushed. Our minds were one. Brian Carson was through running this team. Billy brushed past Brian with what appeared to be a surge of adrenaline. Maybe it was still anger. Maybe it was the hair. He threw his left hand high into the air to catch Henry's attention.

"Henry, over here," Billy called out, lunging forward, dodging between two Preston players as the ball dropped in front of him. He slid his right foot around the ball, scooped it into dribbling position, and took off down the field. He moved quickly back and forth, turning slightly with each forward movement to avoid the one opponent who kept pressing on his left.

I was impressed. I pushed myself down the field, trying to catch up with him, to be there for him. But it was hopeless. My legs already ached, and my heart was pounding in my ears. The goal still looked light-years away. I could hear Coach yelling behind us, his voice only slightly muffled by the shouting and clapping that came from the bleachers. Perhaps Loudmouth Lockwood was yelling for Billy, too, perhaps encouraging him on. That would be a first. Somewhere off to my left, I heard Brian's voice shrieking commands.

"Pass the ball, Jackson; c'mon, pass the ball."

Pass the ball? Pass the ball to who? No one was in passing position. Billy must have heard Brian, too, because I saw him look quickly to the left and then right and then slightly over his left shoulder. He must have had the same question. Pass the ball where?

A shot of energy leaped through my body as I ran forward, PJ to the rescue, my cleats pressing into the muddy patches beneath my feet. Billy saw me, but it was too late. He had been thrown off guard by Brian's voice, and I had only contributed to the disaster. He was doomed as a blur of orange and black surrounded him almost instantly. Legs were flailing forward and backward and sideward and, suddenly, a body came crashing backward in front of me. In the next second, I was flat on the ground.

"Hey, ref. Hey, ref. Yellow card. Yellow card. Illegal slide tackle! Unnecessary roughness. C'mon. C'mon. Let's be fair here."

The harshness of the voice hurt my ears, and as I opened my eyes, I saw Coach and the ref standing upside down, face-to-face. I rolled over and raised myself up onto my knees, inhaling deeply through my nose to catch my breath. I looked between the legs of the guys who had gathered in a small group ten or fifteen feet in front of me. There on the ground lay Billy, groaning. I pushed myself to my feet and winced at the pain as my ankle rebelled against my weight. I hobbled over to the group just as

Brian pushed his way through the players from both teams who had gathered to see what had happened.

"C'mon, Jackson, shake it off. Let's get this game going."

Brian's voice was filled with disgust, and as he threw his foot forward to kick Billy back into action, Henry grabbed his jersey and pulled him backward. It was the bravest thing I'd ever seen Henry do.

"Leave him alone, Carson," Henry said quietly. "Give him some room. Give him a moment to catch his breath."

Brian wheeled around. "Get your hands off me, wuss."

Henry shrugged his shoulders and pushed past him, dropping onto his knees beside his friend. He reached out and touched Billy's shoulder lightly. "You all right, Billy?"

Billy moaned in response.

"Hey, forty-seven, you okay?" one of the Preston players asked as he stepped cautiously toward Billy. "You okay?" Suddenly he jumped back. "Holy shit, somebody get an ambulance."

His swearing caught everyone off guard. Lockwood was pretty clear about language in a game. Don't say anything that could get us a penalty, at least not loud enough for a ref to hear.

As I hobbled closer, Coach dropped his argument with the referee and pushed his way through the crowd gathering around his injured player. There he was, ready to take charge. "C'mon, everyone, back away here. Give my guy some air."

He took one look at Billy and his swaggering evaporated. He stopped dead in his tracks as his eyes traveled from Billy's head down over his body, stopping halfway down Billy's leg. His mouth fell open, but for the first time, for my ears at least, Loudmouth Lockwood found no words. I looked from Coach to Billy, and a knot tightened in my stomach. There it was, a piece of bone poking sharply out the side of Billy's left leg. Not much blood. Just bone sticking out like a baseball bat stuck deep into a snowbank. I suddenly felt like throwing up.

"Call the ambulance!" Coach hollered to someone on the sideline and then knelt down beside Billy, talking quietly, but firmly, asking him how he felt, who he was, where he was. The few of us still left on the field backed away, partly to get out of the way for Mr. Moyer, the assistant coach, who was bringing the first-aid kit, and partly in amazement. It was a side of Coach Lockwood we had never seen. He was quiet. He was calm. He was concerned. We were in awe.

"Okay, guys, c'mon now. Back away." Brian Carson's voice pierced the air harshly, arrogantly. "C'mon. Back away. Give Coach some room here."

I wanted to punch him. He wasn't concerned for Billy. Besides, we had already backed away.

"Shut up, asshole." The words flew out of my mouth.

"Who the hell d'ya think you are, Barnes," he barked in my face as he pushed against my left shoulder with the flat palm of his right hand.

"Get your hands off me, asshole," I shot back as I stumbled backward, wincing with pain as my full weight, all one hundred and thirty-four pounds of it, pressed onto my injured ankle.

Brian's face was purple. He reached out with both hands and grabbed my jersey, pulling me forward, his face no more than six inches from mine. If I could have thought quickly enough, I would have spit in his face. Of course I would have been dead by now if I had.

"Barnes! Carson! Knock it off. Go sit down and cool off!" The voice was loud, but the message was clear. It was Coach.

Brian and I were the only ones left near the collision site, the other players having mysteriously vanished from the field, reappearing on the sidelines and in the bleachers. Only Henry and Coach Lockwood remained. Henry sat on the ground beside his friend while Lockwood squatted near Billy's legs. Coach's mouth was turned downward in a scowl, and he was shaking his head from side to side. I felt like dirt.

Brian flicked me away as though he were flinging dirt from his hands. I fell back once more in pain.

"Sorry, Coach, lost my head," he hollered in his best sucking-up tone of voice. But for me he had a different message. "This ain't over, you puny little shit," he whispered as he brushed by me, heading toward the bench.

Chapter Nine

Frank picked up the phone after the first ring. He listened for just a moment after his mumbled "hello" and then waved the receiver in the air toward me.

"Hello?" I spoke quietly into the phone. I was prepared for gloomy news.

"Hey, PJ." It was Henry. "Everything's cool. Billy's going to live."

That observation was perhaps a little unnecessary. When Billy was taken off the field, he was very much alive, waving lightly from the stretcher as the small crowd in the bleachers clapped on and on.

"That's good, Henry. But will he walk again?"

"Sure. Sure. The nurse said it looked worse than it was. They put a cast on already, and he'll go home tomorrow. Not bad, huh?"

"You seen him?"

"Nah. They only let his family in his room. His mom said she'd have let me in if she was on duty, but she wasn't. It's okay, though. She told him I'm here."

"I'm sure he liked that." I *was* sure. Henry and Billy have been friends forever.

"I gotta go, PJ. See you at school."

"Yeah, sure, Henry," I mumbled as I hung up the phone.

Henry wasn't going to see me at school. I wasn't going. And I had two good reasons: Brian Carson and Mrs. Jordan, Mrs. *Clarice* Jordan.

When I'd gotten home from the game, my mother was waiting for me, armed with information destined to make my life miserable. I hadn't even managed to tell her that Billy was on his way to the hospital, that my friend was on his deathbed, that he might never walk again, before she went up one side of me and down the other about *the* phone call she got at work. She does not like getting phone calls at work. Especially about me. Especially if I'm in trouble. Which apparently I was.

I was supposed to stay after school with Mrs. Jordan, but I didn't. I guess I could say I had the soccer game to worry about, but that wasn't it. I guess you could say I was afraid to see Mrs. Jordan. I had her journal, and I wasn't sure what to do about it. All during English class that morning, I felt like she was looking right through me, like she knew I had that blue notebook. Like maybe she thought I had taken it on purpose.

Life was getting complicated. I hadn't decided what to do about the journal yet, Brian Carson wanted to kill me, and my ankle was still sore from the game. At least I had a reason to stay home from school. As soon as my mom had started yelling, I'd limped across the floor. She fell for the bait and forgot about Mrs. Jordan, at least until after she had examined the ankle, determined it wasn't broken, and suggested a little soaking and an Ace bandage.

Nope, Henry was not going to see me at school. I needed some time to plan my strategy.

"Who was that?" My mother's voice was more demand than question.

"Henry Rose," I answered honestly as I hobbled back to the kitchen, where I had been drying dishes when the phone rang, a small attempt on my mother's part, I think, for us to discuss my current status as after-school detention escapee and general loser. The hobbling was mostly for effect.

"Billy's going to be okay. He might even go home tomorrow," I added, hoping to divert her attention from me.

"I'm glad to hear that. It was nice of Henry to let you know." Her face softened a little. She likes Billy, mostly I think because she works with his mom at the hospital. I think she likes Henry, too, but she also thinks the Roses are stuck-up, that they think they're better than us. Maybe Mr. Rose is, but Henry's just a regular guy.

Her good mood didn't last long.

"Look, PJ. I can't get these phone calls at work anymore."

I thought that was a bit of an exaggeration. She'd only had one other phone call so far this year, after I had skipped math class. Besides, it's not like she'd be in the middle of some big meeting or performing heart surgery or something. She's an aide. So she got interrupted cleaning somebody's bedpan. Big deal.

"When you're done here, you go to your room and do your

homework, especially your English." She paused and looked sideways at me. "Do you have other homework, too?"

I didn't have a clue whether I did or not. It wasn't something I was used to committing to memory. I shrugged my shoulders.

"I don't . . ."

She wouldn't even let me finish. She didn't say anything. She didn't have to. She put her hands on the edge of the sink and stared into the dishwater, her elbows locked. The two seconds of chilling silence were enough.

"Okay, okay, I'll check." I sulked.

We finished the dishes with no more conversation . . . but with no hostility either. Just thick slices of gloom. When the last dish was put away, I laid the wet towel over the edge of the counter and escaped upstairs.

In my room, I flopped down onto my bed. What difference did homework make? I wasn't going to school tomorrow. I knew that. But I did need a plan. Brian Carson and Mrs. Jordan both had to be dealt with. I wasn't really afraid of Brian, but I was pretty sure he could do some serious damage to my body if he wanted to. And Mrs. Jordan? Mostly, she was just a pain in the butt.

I pulled the blue notebook out from underneath the tangled pile of socks in my top drawer. I needed a better place to hide it until I decided what to do. My mother hadn't put my clothes away in years, but you know how mothers are . . . totally unpredictable.

I sat on my bed with Mrs. Jordan's journal in my hands. I'd flipped through it last night. A few things had jumped out at me. Like how she thought the soccer players were stupid for bleaching their hair. And how Henry's father called her and how she told Mr. Cummings, that's our principal, that, yes, she did suggest Henry quit school . . . as a joke. But Mr. Cummings didn't think it was funny. So maybe there was some good stuff there. Who knew? Maybe this was blackmail material. Henry would love it. Imagine me blackmailing Mrs. Jordan. "Hey, Teach, pass me in English or else!" Or else what? Part of me wanted to tear it into a zillion pieces and throw it into the trash. Another part said, *Read on.*

What the hell. Why not? I had no interest in doing homework, especially since I didn't even know what it was, and I sure wasn't going to school the next day.

Chapter Ten

"**. . . and I don't want** another phone call," my mother ordered. Her frustration came through loud and clear. The big sigh was quite unnecessary.

"Yeah, yeah, yeah," I answered as I opened the door, pretending to favor my ankle as I got out of the car, a useless attempt to make my mother feel guilty.

My plan to stay home had flopped. My mother was being Supermom that morning, insisting on dropping me off at school, watching me like a hawk to make sure I entered the building. Parents are dumb like that, aren't they? As though I couldn't walk back out as soon as she drove away. Which I seriously considered doing. But it was too late. Just inside the door was Coach Lockwood, heading upstairs with an armload of papers. He taught social studies. Luckily, I'd never had him for class. The kids who did said he was loud there, too.

"Morning, PJ," he boomed at me from halfway up the stairs. "How's the ankle, bud?"

Apparently, he had forgotten I was the object of his scorn at yesterday's game. Actually, I was pretty surprised that he even remembered I had twisted my ankle. What with Billy's leg and all.

"Pretty sore, Coach." Maybe this could get me out of running laps at practice. "But okay," I added quickly. I couldn't play it up too much. I had quit limping as soon as I entered the building. Lockwood was loud, but he wasn't stupid.

"Glad to hear it. Don't be late to practice," he bellowed as he continued upstairs.

"I gotta stay after for English," I hollered back, standing at the bottom of the stairs looking up at his backside. "For Mrs. Jordan," I added, thinking that little piece of information might carry some weight, considering what I learned about him in her journal: I don't think Barry appreciated the humor of my asking if his team made any touchdowns in Saturday's game. Barry Lockwood didn't have his priorities straight in high school, and he still doesn't.

"I know," he answered, his back still turned toward me. He never missed a step.

He knew? This was just great. Teachers putting their nosy heads together, plotting against me. Quitting the soccer team was looking pretty good.

I glanced up the stairwell as Lockwood reached the second level. As I watched the plaid of his shirt disappear around the corner, I thought once more about taking off. But it was pointless. I was doomed. Everyone was running my life except me.

I dragged myself down the hall to my locker. I had lots of time before first period. My mom had seen to that. I'd thought about heading to the cafeteria, where people hang out in the morning, but I wasn't used to being at school this early and didn't know who would be there. Henry maybe. He was pretty good about getting to school in the morning. *Eldred* saw to that.

So there I was, standing at my locker, trying not to look like someone with nothing to do or no one to talk to. I'd grabbed my Shakespeare book, the first one Mrs. Jordan had given me, from the bottom of the locker and stuffed it into my backpack. At least I'd *appear* to be prepared for class. I'd just stepped back to close the door when the bright yellow metal flew past my eyes and slammed shut, missing my nose by inches.

"So, hey there, P-J-Barnes. What's up?"

Brian Carson leaned his thick forearm against the front of my locker, his right hand propped on his hip. His close-cropped hair made him look older, and probably tougher, than he really was, but with my face inches away from his, he looked tough enough. I didn't care.

"What do you want, Carson?" I was tired of playing games. And the way he mocked my name ticked me off. Was it my fault my mother gave me a stupid nickname that stuck?

"Nobody calls me asshole. You got that?"

He might be surprised at the number of people who called him that.

"Glad to see you're concerned about Billy. He *is* going to be okay. But that news just might disappoint you, huh?" Billy was one of the few sophomores on the team who actually had a little talent, someone Super Athlete here would see as a threat.

"Look, wuss, we are not talkin' about your hotshot friend here. We are talkin' about you and me. Nobody gives me a hard time on the field. I am the captain, and you are nothin'. You got that?"

The color in his face started to darken. He had moved very quickly from bullying to anger. I felt relieved that the hall was starting to fill with other students. Brian liked a show, but he was careful about the audience. I knew I was safe, at least for the moment.

"Hey, guys."

Amanda Cummings peered around from behind the enemy. I'm not sure whether I was glad or annoyed. Brian was thrown off guard, but being saved by a girl is not the quickest way to being cool, especially when she's the principal's daughter.

"Either of you know how Billy is?"

"He's fine," I answered as I turned away and headed for the cafeteria.

"Hey, bud, we're not done here," Brian said in forced-friendly tones.

"I got things to do," I mumbled. I have no idea what Brian did. I just know he didn't follow me. Quitting the team was looking better and better.

"Tell him I said hello," Amanda hollered behind me.

Great. Punching bag for an asshole and errand boy for the love-struck.

Chapter Eleven

"Hey, PJ, over here."

Larry Marston was waving at me from across three rows of cafeteria tables. He was sitting with Kyle Hawkins and Mike Romano.
Kyle was a junior in my sophomore English class and Larry and
Mike were seniors. We weren't friends, and I was a little leery of
anyone who sought out my company. Not too many people did.

"C'mon, c'mon," Larry urged, patting the place on the bench
next to him. "Right here, PJ. We need to talk."

I plopped down across from Mike and eyed the three of
them suspiciously. What was up? They were not looking for my
friendship.

"We were pretty impressed at last night's game," Mike began.

I was impressed that they saw it. These guys were not the type
to hang out after school at the soccer games. They were more likely

to be hanging around the local bar selling drugs. The rumor was that Mike was easy access to marijuana, and Kyle had offered me a toke in the bathroom when I was in eighth grade.

I suddenly felt like an eighth grader again, intimidated by the high schoolers. What was the deal here? I had no money for drugs and had nothing to offer them. But they wanted me. Why?

"Oh yeah?" What would have impressed them at the game? We lost and generally made fools of ourselves on the field.

"Yeah," Larry emphasized. "We liked how you handled Carson."

I almost fell backward off the bench. I had handled that whole situation badly, and they had liked it.

"You did?"

"Yeah, we did," Mike answered, tapping the index finger of his right hand on the table in front of me. "That guy needs an attitude adjustment and just maybe you are the man." He was too sincere. It made me uncomfortable.

"So whadda you guys want?" I asked casually. *Be careful,* my brain said. Not too pushy. Not too friendly.

"We're not sure yet, PJ," Kyle answered, "but Brian Carson owes us something, and we think maybe you can help us get it." His eyes looked wet and glassy, and when they met mine, I turned my attention to the surface of the table. He lowered his voice to almost a whisper. "We just need to know whose side you're on."

I didn't want to be on anybody's side. In fact, being a loner was looking pretty good.

"Look, guys, I gotta go to class." I rose from the bench, lifting one leg out from under the cafeteria table. Larry reached up and grabbed my shoulder, pushing me back to a sitting position. I didn't dare look at him.

"Hey, kid, we're not asking for a favor here. We plan to make good on your help. You get a cut."

"Of what?" I really had no idea what they were talking about.

"Carson owes us money," Mike offered. "We get what we're owed, and you get a cut."

"What does he owe you money for?"

Brian was a jerk, but . . . drugs? I didn't think so. As far as I knew, he didn't even smoke. But what did I know? We weren't exactly in the same social scene.

"You don't need to know. You play with us, we pay."

"How much? And what do I have to do?" What was I saying? These guys were trouble. Everybody knew that. The words in Mrs. Jordan's journal bounced around in my head:

Was Mike Romano a juvenile delinquent in kindergarten? When he passed me in the hall today, and I said, "Good morning," he smiled unctuously and raised his eyebrows like we were partners in some mysterious secret. I'm glad I don't have him again in class. Once was enough.

"O-kay, PJ. Hey, guys, I think we got a player here." Before I could protest, Larry slapped me on the back and hopped up from the bench, adding, "Don't call us; we'll call you."

My stomach twisted into a knot. What had I done?

Just then the warning bell rang for first-period class. Kyle and Mike slowly dragged themselves away from the bench and joined Larry at the end of the table.

"Don't be late for English," Kyle added snidely just before they disappeared around the corner.

The warning bell rang five minutes before first period started. I had plenty of time to get downstairs. Mrs. Jordan's room was the first one on the right. Kyle sat just behind me to the left in class. Kyle and Mrs. Jordan in the same room? Maybe leaving school for the day wasn't a bad idea after all. Maybe I could go to the nurse. Complain about my ankle.

"What are you doing with those guys?"

Henry was standing on the opposite side of the table, books in hand, shaking his head. We had English together first period, but I usually got there just in time for class, if not late. I rarely saw him before class.

"Nothin'."

"They're trouble, PJ."

"Yeah, I know."

"So what's up?"

"Nothin'. They just were talking about the game last night." Telling Henry what just took place didn't seem right. Besides, I didn't know what just took place.

"C'mon, let's go. We'll be late for class," I added. I ditched the plan to get sent home from the nurse's office. It wouldn't work anyway. She'd just call my mom.

"Now I know something's up"—Henry chuckled—"if you're worried about being late for class."

I shrugged my shoulders and picked my backpack up off the table. The two of us headed toward the stairs through halls still filled with students clanging lockers. Only the freshmen were hurrying. I barely remember the beginning of freshman year, but I sure don't remember hurrying anywhere.

Henry and I arrived for English as Mrs. Jordan was closing the door. The bell was just about to ring. Her sense of timing is incredible. That bell rings; that door is closed.

"Morning, Henry. PJ." She stepped aside to let us slide by and then closed the door behind us. "How's Billy, Henry?"

I took note that she addressed her question to Henry. Even she knew Henry and Billy were best friends. I wondered if she knew I was sort of a friend, too.

"Pretty good," Henry responded. "He's coming home today."

"I'm glad to hear that. I guess it wasn't as bad as it looked."

As bad as it looked? Was Mrs. Jordan at the game? Mrs. *Clarice* Jordan came to soccer games? If I treated my students in the classroom the way Barry treats his soccer team, I'd be fired. Maybe she did.

"It sure looked a mess, didn't it? But his mom said it was a pretty clean break."

I stared at Henry as I took my seat. He apparently knew Mrs. Jordan had been at the game.

"How did you know Mrs. Jordan was at the game?" I whispered to him as he slid into the desk to my right.

"You didn't see her?"

I shook my head slightly.

"She comes to a couple games a year," he whispered back to me. "She was standing right next to the bleachers, on the left side."

I stared at him in disbelief. I wouldn't have noticed if she had been carrying a sign that said IT'S MRS. JORDAN; I'M HERE. I guess I never looked much at the spectators. No one was ever there to see me.

A wave of embarrassment fell over me. So Mrs. Jordan had been at the game. She obviously knew I hadn't gone home sick, knew where I had been when I didn't show up after school. Knew I had time to stay after for her and still make the game. No wonder she called my mom at work.

"Henry? PJ?" Mrs. Jordan had started class and demanded our attention. She was walking up and down the aisles, handing back essays. I leaned forward and buried my eyes in the Shakespeare book.

"Many of you did a very nice job with the essay. You took different approaches, and that made them very enjoyable to read. If you do not receive a paper back, it is obviously because you did not submit one. Therefore, I expect you will stay after school today to work on it."

That was me. Of course it didn't make any difference to me, since I was expected to stay anyway. I kept my eyes glued on the donkey's head on the cover of the book in front of me.

"Pssst. PJ?" It was Henry. As I glanced up to see him grinning, he slid a paper over in front of me. It was the letter he had written asking Mrs. Jordan for an extension on his essay:

Interesting approach, Henry. I knew there was a student in there somewhere. Grade: A-

I rolled my eyes and dropped my head onto my desk. For cryin' out loud! That was no essay. It was a stupid letter. Well, I admit it was a pretty good letter. But it was still no essay. Why does everything good always happen to other people?

"Are you all right, PJ?"

I lifted my head and then slouched back in my seat.

"Just great, Mrs. Jordan, just great." I really didn't mean to sound touchy, but that's how I heard myself. A couple students laughed quietly. Kyle Hawkins poked me with his pencil.

"Way to go, Barnes," he teased.

Mrs. Jordan ignored him. She was perched on her stool, her copy of A *Midsummer Night's Dream* in her hand. She hadn't opened it yet. Instead, she took a deep breath and moved her eyes across the class from one side of the room to the other.

"Before we continue with our work, class, I do have something I need to ask you." She paused, and I was sure she was looking right at me. I once more found that picture of the donkey on the cover very interesting. Someone had drawn circles around its eyes, connecting them to look like blue-ink glasses.

"I am missing an important notebook, and I was hoping someone in class had seen it." She paused. "It looks like this, but it has my name in the corner."

I didn't look up. I didn't need to. I knew what it looked like. We waited three very long seconds. I heard Henry clear his throat. *Please, Henry,* I thought, *don't say anything. Don't be clever.* I had considered telling Henry about having the journal. I was glad I hadn't. I glanced over to my right just as a voice slightly behind me spoke. It was Kyle.

"Sorry, Mrs. Jordan. Guess no one's seen it." His voice was not unkind, but the tone revealed his indifference.

"No one?"

I straightened up slowly in my seat just in time to see several kids shrugging their shoulders. Of course no one had seen it. Nobody knew where it was. Just me. And what was I supposed to do now? Raise my hand and say, "Hey there, Mrs. Jordan, I have it. Sorry about that. Just forgot to bring it back to you." That might have made sense before, but now?

"Mrs. Jordan?"

My subliminal plea to Henry had failed.

"Yes, Henry?"

"How about a reward?" He paused briefly. "You know, like some points on our average or something?"

The class laughed.

"Well, Henry, maybe we can work something out," Mrs. Jordan answered. "You know where it is?" The tone of her voice said she presumed Henry was joking. She clearly didn't know the bargain he had made with his father was about his grades.

"No, but for ten points, I'll look."

"Fifteen," Kyle countered, probably figuring that was how much he needed to pass.

"Okay, that's enough," Mrs. Jordan said, taking control before the bidding took off further. "If anyone finds it, I would appreciate its return." She tossed the notebook onto an empty desk and opened her book. "On to Mr. Shakespeare. Let's begin on page 197. Jennie, you be Titania; Henry, be Cobweb; Robert, read Mustardseed, please; and, PJ, you take the role of Bottom."

Great. I got to be the ass.

Chapter Twelve

"Hey, Barnes! Need a ride home?" Larry was leaning out the passenger-side window of the dark blue Mustang that had pulled up alongside the curb. Mike was sitting behind the wheel. "C'mon. We'll drop your friend off, too."

Henry and I had just left practice and were almost to the end of School Street. We'd missed the sports bus that would have dropped us off at the center of town, but neither one of us lived too far to walk all the way from school. Still, daylight was disappearing quickly, and our sweaty bodies made the air seem even colder. A souped-up Mustang was pretty inviting. If it hadn't been Larry Marston and Mike Romano in the front seat, neither one of us would have hesitated.

"C'mon. C'mon. Get in," Larry urged.

I looked at Henry, but he wouldn't look at me. Larry and Mike were definitely not on Eldred Rose's list of acceptable friends.

"Well, Henry, what d'ya think? Ride in a cool car for half a mile?"

Henry's eyes met mine as he shook his head from side to side. "You go on if you want to, PJ. I'll walk." He shifted his backpack from his right shoulder to his left and continued down the sidewalk.

I felt trapped. Henry was right. These guys were trouble. But, hey, it's not like Henry and I were best friends. As soon as Billy was back on his feet, I'd be in the backseat again anyway. I guess backseat in a Mustang wasn't too shabby.

"C'mon, Rosey, you too good to ride in an old junker like this?" Larry's voice was filled with sarcasm as he hollered up the street toward Henry. "Maybe Daddy'll buy you something better when you're old enough to drive."

I had to give Henry credit. He never looked back.

Larry hopped out and pulled the front seat forward. I threw my backpack onto the backseat and climbed in. Larry hardly had the door closed when Mike took off.

"You guys know where I live?"

Mike laughed. "Of course we know where you live, Barnes."

Obviously Mike thought it was a stupid question. I didn't think so. I didn't know where either of them lived. As we sped by Henry, Larry shot his arm out the window and raised his middle finger.

"Henry's okay," I offered.

Larry turned around slightly in his seat. "Rose is a jerk. But you, PJ, you are the man."

Yeah, right.

At the end of School Street, Mike turned left on Main, but instead of heading straight through town, he turned on to the first side street and pulled over to the curb. He put the car in park and pulled out a pack of Marlboros, took one out, and then offered the pack to me.

"No thanks," I said. He shrugged his shoulders and tucked the pack back into his shirt pocket. I felt a tightening in my stomach. I wasn't in any danger with these guys. I hadn't done anything to them. At least not that I knew. But something was up. I sat tight and waited for them to make the first move.

"Okay, Barnes, here's the deal," Mike began, looking at me in the rearview mirror. He paused, taking a long drag on his cigarette and blowing a cloud of smoke out the window.

All this time, I had thought it was Larry Marston who ran the show. Larry was bigger and taller than Mike. When he and Mike and Kyle Hawkins walked through the halls, it was Larry who drew the attention. He was pretty good-looking, I guess. At least I knew all the girls flirted with him. Even Heather. Kyle looks a lot like Larry, tall and thin, but he isn't as smooth as Larry. Mike is shorter and darker and quieter. As I sat in the backseat wondering what mess I'd gotten myself into, it became clear that Mike was the real leader. He transferred the cigarette from his right hand to his left and shifted in his seat to face me.

"Carson owes us money, and you're gonna help us get it," Mike explained, repeating what he had said that morning in the cafeteria. "And here's how." He gave a slight nod to Larry, who had turned to face me.

"You go see him," Larry continued. "Tell him you know he's

using steroids. Tell him if he doesn't come up with the money he owes us, three hundred and fifty bucks, you're gonna tell Lockwood."

I stared straight ahead, trying not to look directly at either of them. But I didn't need to look in their eyes to know this was no joke. It was pretty sharp thinking on their part. Playing soccer meant more to Brian than anything. Steroids? Maybe. But that's a football thing, not soccer. Still, he'd do anything if he thought it would help him. It didn't have to make sense.

"Well?" Larry urged.

"I'm thinking."

I was thinking. How did I let myself get sucked into this? On the other hand, Brian was a jerk, and if he was really on drugs, why should I care what happened to him?

"What's there to think about?" Mike asked as he put his arm out the window and flicked the ashes from his cigarette into the street.

"What makes you think it will work? If he hasn't got the money now, where's he gonna get it? I sure don't know where I'd get three hundred and fifty dollars."

"We think he's got it," Larry explained, "and just figures he can shaft us."

That sounded like Brian. These guys were low-life, manipulators and schemers, maybe even guilty of some shoplifting or petty theft, but as far as I knew, they never used physical force. They didn't need to. Their presence was intimidating all by itself. They were probably right. The Carsons weren't as rich as the Roses, but Brian always seemed to have money. And he was just arrogant enough to think he could get away without paying them. What were they going to do? Go to the police? Still, where did I fit in?

"So why should I care? Why don't *you* tell him you're going to Lockwood? Why me?"

Mike turned farther around in his seat so that he was looking directly into my eyes. His mouth twitched at one corner, and when he spoke, his voice was quiet but clear.

"Because you, Barnes, have credibility," he explained slowly, emphasizing his last syllable. "Lockwood would not want to hear bad things about his star player. He'd find it very easy to ignore us, presume we were just causing trouble for Carson. But you? He'd believe you."

Credibility? That was a first. These guys must have searched long and hard to come up with that explanation.

"You gotta be kidding," I blurted out. "Brian Carson and I just blew up at each other in a game, and you think Lockwood is going to believe anything I say about him?"

"Actually," Mike continued slowly, "it doesn't matter what Lockwood thinks. It matters what Carson thinks. And Carson will think you are just pissed off enough to go through with it. And if Carson thinks you have credibility with the coach, then that's all that matters."

That caught my attention. Would Brian really think Coach would believe me? A feeling of power swept through my body.

"What makes you think I won't just tell Lockwood anyway?"

"You can tell Lockwood anything you damn well please . . . after Carson pays up," Mike answered hotly.

"What about you? What if I tell him the whole story?"

Power. It has a way of making you feel unusually brave.

"You don't know the whole story," Larry snapped as he

settled back into his seat so that he was once again facing forward. "And that jerk just might believe you, but where's the proof? One person's word against another's. Besides, you wouldn't be stupid enough to get us involved . . . would you, Barnes?"

They were right. I probably wouldn't.

"Forty bucks," Larry added. "That's your cut when he pays." He paused, a slow smile forming on his face like he'd just thought of something funny. "When was the last last time you had forty bucks, Barnes?"

I had never had forty bucks in my hands at one time in my life. Forty bucks for a conversation. They weren't asking me to buy or sell drugs, just pass along some information.

"I gotta think about this."

"Well, don't think too long," Mike answered as he started up the engine and pulled away from the curb. "We're counting on Carson worrying about sectionals."

"Easy money for you, PJ," Larry added, his voice serious. "This should not be a tough decision."

We rode the rest of the way in silence. I wondered if that was supposed to be my thinking time. Did they expect an answer when we reached my house? I hoped not. I didn't have one.

As Mike swung into the driveway, Frank was coming out of the garage carrying a can of oil. He was always putting oil in his truck. Larry leaned his head out the window and hollered loudly to him.

"Hey there, Frank, what's up?"

Frank stopped by the front of his truck and lifted his right hand in a slight wave as Larry opened the door and hopped out. I grabbed my backpack and stepped out onto the driveway.

"Talk to ya later," Larry whispered to me as I brushed past him. He slid back into the car and once more stuck his head out the window, flashing a big smile and raising his right hand in a wave. "Hang in there, Frank."

Mike never said a word.

"You know those guys?" I asked Frank as the two of us stood watching the back of the Mustang speed down the street.

"They friends of yours?"

"Not really. They just gave me a ride."

"They've been in the shop a few times," he offered.

I guess that was supposed to answer my question. I don't know whether it did or not.

"I'd stay away from them," he added.

I hadn't made that decision yet.

Chapter Thirteen

"PJ!" My mother's voice came with four sharp raps on my bedroom door. "It's almost eleven. Get up."

Eleven . . . my mother's idea of sleeping late.

"Go away," I mumbled, pulling the pillow over my head.

"PJ?"

"I heard you," I moaned.

Every Saturday morning she had a list of jobs for me to do. This morning the list would probably be longer than usual. It had not been a smooth week in the Barnes household.

"You movin'?"

"Yes, yes, yes," I snapped. I hadn't yet opened my eyes.

"Don't get snotty with me, young man. Just get up and get going."

I buried my head deeper.

"You hear me?" she added.

"I'm up," I growled back.

"Downstairs. Ten minutes." One more rap on the door.

I pulled my head out from under the pillow and rolled over onto my back, staring at the light fixture on my ceiling. The single bulb glared back. As I stretched out my arms and legs to unstiffen from the night's sleep, I realized how uncomfortable I was, having slept in my clothes. I rolled over on my side and looked at the clock: 10:58. I swung my legs off the bed and pushed myself to a sitting position.

I rolled my head around, trying to loosen the stiffness. As it dropped down onto my chest for the third time, I opened my eyes. Staring up at me from between my feet was Mrs. Jordan's blue notebook, spread open, facing downward onto the floor.

My heart started to pound as a wave of panic swept over me. I grabbed it up and smoothed out the pages, glancing quickly around the room as though I expected someone to appear at the window or burst through the door at any moment.

"PJ," my mother hollered again, this time from the bottom of the stairs.

"Damn," I whispered to myself as I shoved the notebook under my pillow.

"PJ!"

"I'm up. I'm up," I yelled back through the closed door.

I stood beside my bed, staring at the pillow. This was stupid. Did I think my mother would be suspicious of a damn notebook? We had an understanding, she and I, that my room was my mess. But I suddenly had visions of her deciding to change the sheets on my bed or paint the ceiling or look for bombs. She was so pissed at me about the phone call from school that nothing would have surprised me. Besides, I'd already decided to return the notebook Monday morning.

My halfhearted effort to do homework last night was a last-ditch attempt to convince my mother to sign my working papers. But I couldn't get into it. So instead, I looked through Mrs. Jordan's journal again. Why? I'm not sure. She wrote mostly about the kids at school. But no dirt. Nothing useful. Except maybe what she thought about Carson, which sort of surprised me: If corporal punishment were still allowed in public schools, I would have dropped Brian Carson in his tracks right there in the hall today. One swift clip to the side of the head and, bam, watch one hundred and ninety pounds of obnoxious muscle crumple.

I wondered what Carson did to tick her off. Not that it would have taken much . . . on his part or hers. But most of what I'd read was pretty boring. Which is probably why it put me to sleep.

So on Monday morning I would give it back to her. It was the only way out of the trap I was in. I couldn't keep it and I couldn't bring myself to trash it. English class every day for the rest of the year? Guilt every day? No way! I'd tell her it was with the things she'd given me that night after school and that I hadn't looked at that stuff until the weekend. She'd believe that. It was close to the truth. Or maybe I'd just sneak in and leave it on her desk.

I pulled the notebook out from under the pillow and slipped it into my backpack. I would keep my guilt close to me. The other stuff she'd given me had fallen off my bed and was all over the floor. I left it. It looked more normal.

"'Bout time," my mother greeted me as I entered the kitchen.

She was sitting at the table, sorting through papers, a pad and pen in front of her. She looked up at me with raised eyebrows.

"You look like you slept in your clothes," she added.

There was no annoyance in her voice. Maybe a little exasperation. Yet I was surprised she noticed at all. It's not like I had never slept in my clothes before.

"I did," I mumbled as I stared into the refrigerator. I wasn't particularly hungry, but my mouth felt like cotton. Probably from the corn chips I had eaten last night just before I fell asleep. I needed juice or milk or something. I spotted a pitcher of Kool-Aid. That would do. I lifted the pitcher and glugged down several mouthfuls.

"For cryin' out loud, PJ. Do you think you could use a glass?"

Now she sounded annoyed.

I grabbed a glass from the dish drainer, filled it three times with the purple liquid, and downed every drop without saying a word. I left the empty glass on the counter and put the pitcher back into the refrigerator.

"There, you happy?" I snarled as I swung the door closed.

"No, PJ, I am not happy. I am not happy at all. Do you think maybe you could just be civil? I certainly wouldn't ask for pleasant. I guess pleasant would be too much."

Well, I'd done it. Now she was pissed.

Brrriinngggg. My mother dropped the pen onto the table and pushed her chair back, reaching for the phone on the wall as she rose. She answered it before the second ring.

"Hello?"

She listened for a moment and then held the phone out for

me without a word. She sat back down at the table as I took the phone.

"Hey," I began, "what's up?" I had no idea who was on the other end. It didn't matter. The ring had saved me from another lecture.

The caller couldn't have been better.

"It's Billy, Mom. He said it's okay to come over." I purposely left my hand off the receiver as I spoke to her. Parents usually don't like sounding cranky in front of your friends.

I had called Billy the night before to see how he was doing. The truth is, I had been looking for an excuse to get out of the house. Not that I wasn't concerned about him. I was. But I had been more concerned about being grounded on a Friday night. My mom liked Billy. If he had been ready for visitors, even she'd have given in. But Mrs. Jackson said no, maybe in the morning.

"Did you get your homework done last night," my mother asked mechanically, pen in hand once more, staring at the pile of papers in front of her.

"Most of it," I lied.

"What about your chores?" The list was already taped to the cupboard.

"Later?"

She looked up at me and shrugged. She was giving in. Maybe it was giving up. Either way worked for me. She lifted her right hand from where it rested on the table and waved it aimlessly in the air.

"Be over in ten minutes," I replied to Billy. I hung the phone up quickly and headed toward the stairs, pausing for just a moment in the doorway.

"Thanks," I said to my mother, trying to sound like I meant it. I really did. She looked up and smiled, but her face was all scrunched up, more like she was trying not to cry. Our brief argument wasn't that bad. For a moment I thought about calling Billy back. But I didn't.

I hustled up to my room to change my shirt and throw a Jackie Chan video into my backpack. I didn't want my mother to have second thoughts. I was about to escape out my door when I spied the scattered homework on the floor and scooped it up and into my backpack. I had already lied to her about it being done. No sense taking the chance she might find it abandoned on my floor. Why give the enemy ammunition? In less than a minute, I was on my way back downstairs.

"Don't you think you ought to at least comb your hair," she snapped as I hurried through the kitchen. She was still sitting at the table, still staring at the pile of papers. She really didn't even look at me, so I'm not sure how she knew I hadn't.

"It's okay," I replied. I was trying to be nice. I really was. "Billy doesn't care what I look like."

She gave a big sigh. "I go to work at three, PJ. Frank'll be home by five. No trouble, okay?"

"No trouble, Mom. I'll stay at Billy's. I promise."

Chapter Fourteen

"So, you in big trouble?"

Billy lay on his unmade bed chewing a Twizzler, his left leg propped up on a pillow. He looked pretty good, considering two days ago we all thought he was dead.

"Nah. Not really." It was probably the truth. I hadn't done anything illegal. "I don't think I'll go to jail for not doing homework and skipping out on Mrs. Jordan."

Billy laughed. I liked it that he thought I was a tough kid. I wondered if Henry told him about me taking off with Larry and Mike. I'm not really tough, but I am compared to him. Except for an occasional flare-up of temper, usually in defense of someone else, which I might add got him his broken leg, Billy is a pretty calm guy. Me? I'm always a little touchy. He smiles and laughs a lot. I snarl and sulk. You'd think we'd rub off on each other a little.

"Maybe you're going to be suspended. Wouldn't that be cool? Permission to stay home." His eyes stared off into space as though he were planning how he, too, could become a truant. His observations were pretty funny coming from a guy who now had a perfectly good reason not to go to school.

"I doubt it. I haven't skipped all that much."

I removed the CDs from the player and inserted three different ones. Billy's family isn't as rich as the Roses, but he has even more stuff than Henry. With a broken leg, he'll probably be even more spoiled.

"Besides," I continued as I put the discs back into their cases, "Mr. Cummings thinks I'm deranged. He told my mom once I needed counseling." I crossed my eyes and shook my head violently. Billy laughed.

"You wanta go down to Pete's?" he asked. "I'll buy."

This guy is amazing. Nothing ever gets him down. Two days before, his leg was a twisted mess, but there he was willing to hobble downtown to entertain a friend. That's Billy. Spoiled, yes. Selfish, no.

I shook my head.

"I better not. My mom wasn't too wild about my coming over here. If she sees me there on her way to work, I'll be dead." I grabbed the Twizzler out of Billy's hand. "This will have to do." I needed to change the subject. I didn't want him to think I was weak. He thought I was a rebel, and I preferred to keep it that way.

"You want the Jackson germs, you're welcome to them. Here, have some more." He flung the half-empty bag at me. "They come with a mangled leg, though." He laughed, but the sigh that followed showed his frustration.

"Tough way to end the season, huh, Billy?"

He slowly eased his legs off the bed and lifted himself up onto his crutches. He moved like he had used them for years. All that serious practice time for soccer was paying off, in a morbid sort of way.

"I'll live. C'mon, let's watch a movie." He swung himself across the room and through the doorway. "Besides, real food awaits us in the kitchen."

Two microwave pizzas and one movie later, there we were, Billy stretched out on the sofa and me on the floor. The pizza had been fair, the movie slightly better. Billy was flipping through the channels on the remote, from golf to weather to rebuilding old houses. The afternoon was looking pretty dull.

As I stood up to take my empty plate to the kitchen, I thought about heading home, not that there was anything more exciting to do there, but only because I was getting pretty bored. But then again, sometimes just doing nothing is okay. Billy and I were a good match for energy level. Billy punching numbers on the remote and me punching numbers on the microwave was the peak of our physical activity for the day.

While I was in the kitchen rinsing off my plate, something I never did at home but always did at the Jacksons', the phone rang.

"You want me to answer it?" I yelled as I wiped my hands on my jeans. By this time it was on its second ring.

"I got it," Billy hollered back just as the third ring began. When I stepped into the doorway between the dining room and the family room, I saw Billy stretched out over the end of the sofa, talking into the phone that sat on his father's desk. His right leg was pulled up under him for support with his injured leg stretched out straight, his foot resting on the floor. He looked extremely uncomfortable.

"Yeah, he's here," Billy answered into the phone as he looked straight at me. "No kidding? Yeah, yeah, I'll tell him." He turned his eyes away from mine and stared at the floor. "Okay. Yeah, I will." He dropped the receiver into place and slid back down onto the sofa.

"Well?" I asked. "My mom looking for me?"

"That was my mom. Your mother's at the hospital."

"Yeah? What's up? What does she want?" I could hear the edge in my voice. I didn't need my mother checking up on me.

"She's *in* the hospital, PJ." Billy spoke slowly and quietly, stressing the word *in*. "She had an accident on the way to work."

The muscles in my stomach tightened.

"And . . . ?" I moved forward into the room. Billy grabbed the remote and turned off the TV.

"She's hurt pretty bad. My mom's trying to find Frank. You need to get down there right away."

The tension in my stomach started crawling upward into my throat. I felt like crying. I felt like yelling. I felt like a jerk.

"Take my bike," Billy offered. "It's just inside the garage."

"Thanks, Billy. I will."

I ran up to Billy's bedroom and grabbed my backpack. By the time I came down, he was in the kitchen, pressing the garage-door opener for me.

"I hope she's okay, PJ," he called after me as I flew past him out the back door.

"Me, too," I whispered to myself as I jumped down the porch steps.

Chapter Fifteen

I pumped as fast as I could, but the front tire was a little soft and the whole bike felt sluggish. My head felt sluggish, too. I wanted to believe that it was probably nothing. After all, we hadn't heard any sirens that afternoon. If there had been a really bad accident, wouldn't we have heard sirens? Even with the television blaring, surely we would have heard an ambulance. Wouldn't we?

I chugged my way down Maple Avenue, the bike growing heavier and heavier with each push of the pedals. The hospital was only about a mile across town from Billy's house. Still, I thought I was never going to get there. By the time I reached the intersection with East Main, I dumped the bike on someone's lawn and took off running. It had to be faster. My heart pounded in my head and my lungs gasped for air with each step. So much for soccer training.

I reached the center of town just as the traffic light switched to green. I stopped at the curb, leaned forward, and put my hands on my knees, trying to catch my breath.

"PJ," a voice boomed to my right. "Get in."

Frank was leaning out the window of his pickup truck as he waited at the intersection for the light to change. I hustled across the street and around the front of the truck. The light in his lane had already turned green by the time I reached the passenger-side door, and Frank released the clutch as I swung the door closed. We lurched through the intersection just as the car behind us blared its horn.

"Bastard," Frank muttered as he threw his left hand out the window and waved his middle finger.

"Mrs. Jackson call you?" I asked.

"She called the shop and left a message with Ernie. I was out road-testing a car." He paused and glanced briefly in my direction. "I thought you were grounded."

Frank worked at Ernie's Auto Repair, or at least he had for the past three months. He never keeps a job for very long, but he always manages to be working somewhere, mostly at garages or repair shops.

"Not really."

I was surprised he remembered, or even cared, that my mom was on my case this week. When my mom and I argued, Frank generally shrugged his shoulders and walked away. I was not his problem. Sure enough, as we sat in the cab of his truck heading to the hospital, he shrugged his shoulders and fell into silence.

Frank turned right at the next block and swung left immediately into the hospital parking lot. He pulled into the first empty spot and slammed on the brakes. We were both out of the truck before it had come to a complete stop. The Bradford Community Hospital was pretty small. Even the two entrances, one for emergencies and the other for visitors and people who had appointments for blood tests and stuff like that, were less than fifty feet apart. We headed for the nearest door, the one for visitors, and bolted inside.

There is no real lobby to the hospital, just a small room with a few chairs and a couple end tables. Opposite the entrance is another door to the main hallway. Next to that doorway is a small glassless window where a lady sits at a desk directing visitors and patients to wherever they need to go.

Frank stopped at the window.

"How is she, Margie?" he asked, his hands pressed against the bottom edge of the window opening.

"I really don't know," the voice answered quietly. "A nurse will be out soon. Why don't you sit down?"

Frank pushed himself away from the window and plunked down into the chair nearest the entrance to the hall. I couldn't sit. I paced. Back and forth, back and forth. Ten feet to the hallway, ten feet back to the entrance, ten feet to the hallway, ten feet back to the entrance.

"For chrissakes, PJ, sit down," Frank barked at me.

"I don't want to," I growled back.

"Well, it's damned annoying."

I didn't answer him, and I didn't sit down. Being annoying was my best skill.

One hundred and forty-two paces later, a nurse appeared in the doorway.

"Hello, Frank. Hi, PJ. Why don't you come with me?"

It was Mrs. Baker. She lives near us and sometimes even gives my mom a ride to work if they're working the same shift. She's a real nurse, not like my mom or Billy's mom, who are just aides.

We followed her down the hall and into a lounge next to the cafeteria. Several people were eating at the few tables in the dining area, but no one was in the lounge.

"C'mon in here," Mrs. Baker urged, "where we can—"

"How's my mom, Mrs. Baker? Is she going to be all right?" My voice was shaking.

"Sit down, PJ," Frank interrupted, "and take it easy. Let her talk."

"Leave me alone, Frank. What do you care anyway?" I wasn't making sense, but I didn't care. I have this talent for saying the wrong thing at the wrong time.

"PJ, sit down." Mrs. Baker's voice was calm and quiet but firm. I threw myself into a chair next to the door. Mrs. Baker sat in the chair next to me. Frank pulled up a chair so that he faced the two of us.

"Your mom is going to be fine," she began. "She is badly injured, but it wasn't necessary to have her airlifted to Syracuse. That's a good sign. Dr. Spencer's with her right now. He's very good, PJ."

I nodded slightly, looking at my feet. I did know who Dr. Spencer was, but only by name. I didn't think I'd ever seen him, and I didn't know whether he was good or not.

"How bad?" Frank asked, edging forward in his chair.

It was a good question, a fair question. But I rose in my seat, feeling the blood rise to my head. I wanted to punch him. For no good reason. I think I was angry because I hadn't asked it.

"Her left arm and left leg are broken. She has a lot of bruising, and she's being checked for internal bleeding and to make sure there's no damage to her vital organs. It will be a while. You wait here, and I'll let you know what's happening."

Her bluntness was startling. Maybe she saw the tension between me and Frank and was putting the focus back on my mom. It worked, at least for the moment. Frank and I just stared at her.

"I'm sorry, PJ," she said as she put her hand on my arm.

"What happened?" Frank asked, sitting on the edge of his chair. "Where did it happen?"

"I'm not really sure. I just know it was up by Midtown Market. I heard the state police were on the scene. They'll probably be around to talk to you."

"For chrissakes, Frank, does it matter?" Once more, I wanted to slug him. I might have if Mrs. Baker hadn't stood up and put her hand firmly on my shoulder.

"What matters, PJ, is that you stay calm. You need to do that for your mother. You hear me?"

I shrugged and sank back into the chair.

"I'll be back as soon as I have some news."

Frank stood up and nodded as she left the room. He stood there, staring after her for a long time, and then sat back down and put his head in his hands. He heaved a long sigh and his shoulders began shaking. It was pretty weird. I never thought about him actually caring about my mom. I mean, I know he must have cared about her, or they wouldn't have gotten married, but I never saw much evidence of it. They didn't fight, but he never said nice things to her, and I don't think I'd ever seen them kiss.

I cleared my throat. He didn't take the hint.

"Frank? You okay?" It was pretty hard to stay mad at someone who was falling apart on you. He rolled his head back and forth in his hands. I took that for a no.

"Frank?"

He dropped his hands into his lap and took a deep breath as he sat back in the chair and turned his head to look at me. His eyes are an eerie blue, the kind that seem to look through you. Maybe that's why I had never really looked at him. Maybe I thought he saw a *me* I didn't want him to see. He was an intruder, and he and I both knew I resented him from the first moment he showed up in our house.

"Doesn't sound too good, does it?"

His tone startled me. He didn't sound like the Frank who barely mumbled hello when I saw him, grumbled about money whenever he heard me asking my mom for anything, or swore under his breath when he was working on his truck. He sounded like a real human being speaking to another real human being. And he sounded very worried.

"Mrs. Baker said she'd be fine." I was convincing myself of that as much I was trying to assure Frank.

"I love her, PJ."

That simple statement caught me totally off guard. It also embarrassed me. Nobody in my family ever said that. Nobody.

I wanted to answer him, to tell him I loved her, too. I must have or I wouldn't have been standing there with my heart pounding. But I didn't say a word. I just nodded. I was pretty impressed with myself for not making some smart-ass comment.

Frank leaned forward and pulled a red bandanna out of his

back pocket, blew his nose, and then wadded it up and stuffed it into the right front pocket of his shirt. He cleared his throat and then stood up to stretch.

"You got any money?" he asked, looking through the doorway to the cafeteria.

"You want to eat?"

Our touching moment was apparently gone.

"I could use a cup of coffee. I don't have a cent on me."

That was no surprise. Frank never had any money. At first I thought maybe he spent all his money on drugs. He had really long hair, rode a motorcycle, and smoked way too much when he and my mom got married. The hair stayed, but the motorcycle got replaced by the truck. He even tried to quit smoking several times. I'm still not sure about the drugs. If he knew Mike and Larry, maybe. But I didn't think so. Yet money is always an issue in our house. Probably because there never seems to be any. And I can never figure out why. My mom works. Frank works. Well, at least he has a job most of the time.

"I don't think so," I mumbled as I searched through my pockets. "I think there's some change in my backpack, though. I'll go get it."

I walked slowly down the hall, back through the lobby, and out the door. My head was swimming from the antiseptic smell of the hospital, so I was glad for the excuse to go outside. The air felt cool on my face, and my head began to clear as I walked across the parking lot to the truck. I opened the passenger door and reached across the seat where my backpack had slid forward against the gearshift when Frank stopped abruptly. I had intended to rummage through the outside pocket for the change that I was sure was there, but instead I swung the whole pack out of the truck and over my shoulder. If I wasn't so worried about my mom, and I really was, I would have headed off down the street toward home. My mom's life was in danger, and Frank was falling apart on me. I wasn't handling either very well. I glanced down the street for a moment and then turned back toward the entrance. Frank had probably already purchased coffee on credit in the cafeteria, telling the lady at the cash register that I would be there with the cash soon.

I was right. By the time I was back in the lounge, Frank was leaning back in the chair, coffee cup in hand, steam rising from the top. He glanced up as I entered through the doorway. I guess he was through falling apart.

"Sixty cents," he said as he blew across the top of the cup. "I told the lady you'd be right back."

"What made you think I had sixty cents, Frank? What if I only had fifty?"

He stared at me with such a pained look on his face, I regretted the sarcasm immediately. But he was back to being Frank. Totally irresponsible, expecting my mom to take care of everything. That was it! That was why he had seemed so lost all of a sudden. He was afraid my mother was going to die, and then where would he be? Maybe he does love her. I don't know about that. But I do know he depends on her for everything. I was seeing Frank for the first time as he really was. Just what my mom needed, another kid to take care of. I should have been enough.

"Sorry, Frank. Never mind. I'll take care of it."

I plopped my backpack onto an empty chair and reached into the outside pocket, feeling around the bottom for the loose change

I knew was there. I could feel several coins as I swept my hand around, scooping up what was there. I picked out two quarters and a dime, dropped the rest of the coins into my pants pocket, and walked into the cafeteria to settle Frank's account. I cut through the roped-off section that separates the buyers from the eaters and bypassed two nurses waiting for their orders. I handed the cashier the coins.

"The coffee buyer," I said as I nodded toward the lounge.

"Nothing for you?" she asked in return, which was a lot nicer than Frank's attitude.

I shook my head no and went back to the lounge just as Mrs. Baker was coming in through the hall door. Frank was already on his feet.

"Any news?" he asked as he sipped coffee from the edge of his cup.

"Not really," Mrs. Baker answered. "I just wanted to let you know it will be a while, probably at least two hours, maybe longer."

"Do you know how she's doing?" I asked.

"She'll be fine, PJ. But right now? No, I don't." She turned her attention to Frank. "If you and PJ want to go home, I'll make sure you're called as soon as you can see her. But even then, she'll be pretty heavily sedated for a while."

"We'll be here in the lounge, Mrs. Baker. You can find us here," I answered for the two of us. I didn't trust Frank to make any decisions. Sure he was upset and worried, but it would not have surprised me if he had told Mrs. Baker she could call him at the garage or at home or just about anywhere.

Frank looked at me and bobbed his head up and down.

"PJ's right. We'll be right here."

Mrs. Baker smiled and nodded. "I figured as much." As she turned and left, Frank sat back down and set his coffee on the table beside him.

"Now what?" He sighed. "Just sit here and wait? What do I do for a couple hours besides sit and worry?"

I glanced at my backpack. "Wanta do my homework for me?" Frank just glared at me. My attempt to lighten the mood didn't work. "I was kidding. I was kidding."

I *was* kidding. The thought of Frank doing homework was pretty funny. I guess I had seen him glance at a newspaper once in a while, but not much else, except maybe *Motor Trend* or *Popular Mechanics*. Homework really wasn't on my mind just then, but my poor attempt at a joke stayed in my head as my backpack sat in the chair staring at me. Guilt. I remembered my mom asking me that morning if I had done my homework. Maybe I could do something while I waited. Ease my guilt.

"I'm goin' in there."

Frank's voice startled me. He was on his feet and already halfway to the cafeteria door.

"Frank?"

He paused for a moment and looked over his shoulder at me. "There's a TV," he said, pointing through the door to the opposite corner of the cafeteria as though that answered any question I might have. "You comin'?"

I shook my head no. "I got things I can do here," I said, waving toward my backpack.

"Suit yourself," he replied. "Call me when she comes back."

"I will."

I watched through the opened doorway as he wandered over

to the table beneath the television mounted on the wall. He set his coffee cup down on the table and reached up to turn it on.

Frank had returned to being Frank, and I was glad. I preferred being alone. No one else was in the lounge, and not likely to be. Visitors pretty much came and went as they pleased here. No one ever really had to wait for special hours. My mom said working Saturdays wasn't so bad. They were quiet. No one came in for tests or X-rays or anything like that, and the only surgery would be emergencies.

Like hers.

Chapter Sixteen

Less than an hour had gone by and I had all the busywork done. The vocab sheets were easy. The stuff on Shakespeare was harder. I actually had to skim through Mrs. Jordan's handouts to find the answers. I hadn't paid attention in class lately, and I couldn't remember much from last year when we studied *Romeo and Juliet*, although I did think it was cool that the guy was willing to die for someone he loved. I remember wondering at the time if I would be willing to die for Heather. Of course that was before she dumped me.

I still had the essays to write and zero interest in doing them. My homework energy was gone. But Mrs. Baker had not yet returned, and Frank was still glued to the TV. I pulled my backpack up onto my lap to sort through the mess of remaining papers.

At least I could find the assignments and, well, think about them. I probably didn't have any clean paper with me anyway. Any excuse would do.

I pulled out a stack of papers and then dropped the pack onto the floor. The copy of *Rolling Stone* sitting on top of the pile caught my eye. As I picked it up, an edge of blue stuck out from underneath some of the other papers. My heart jumped. I looked around quickly to see if anyone was watching. I had totally forgotten about the journal.

There I sat with the blue notebook flat in my lap, holding on to the sides with both hands. Last night's look into Mrs. Jordan's head flooded over me. A little guilt. A little curiosity. Perhaps not in that order. I stared at her journal. I had already read far too much. Anything I had read was far too much. And no matter what I told her on Monday when I returned it, she would know I had read it. She just would.

I probably should've shoved it back into my pack. But I didn't have anything to lose. So far I hadn't read anything terribly interesting. Not much I didn't know already, except the stuff about Lockwood. Since I had this new plan to do homework—well, sort of, at least enough to ease my guilt—maybe there was some useful information I hadn't uncovered. Besides, anything was better than writing an essay, for which, I might add again, I had no paper. I opened the front cover and started flipping through the pages, looking to see where I had left off. My name jumped off the page.

. . . PJ Barnes . . .

She wrote about me?

. . . somewhat of a lost soul, like PJ . . .

Lost soul? Mrs. Jordan thought I was a lost soul?

. . . it's no wonder he has a chip on his shoulder . . . Stephanie quitting school two months after PJ was born . . . who could blame her . . . a baby to care for . . . having to deal with Peter Barnes . . . who didn't want to be a husband . . . much less a father . . .

I felt my face burning.

"Peter Barnes?"

I snapped my head around toward the voice, and there stood a gray uniform peering down at me. I closed the notebook and slid it down into my backpack, top first, so that *Clarice Jordan* was out of sight.

"Peter?"

Nobody calls me Peter, but I nodded anyway.

"I'm Trooper Lawrence, Peter. Could I talk to you about your mom's accident?"

"PJ," I answered.

"Huh?"

"Everybody calls me PJ."

"Okay, then, PJ it is. And your dad, PJ? I was told he was in here with you."

"Stepdad," I explained. "Frank is not my father."

Obviously everyone knew my real dad was a loser, even Mrs. Jordan, but I was not about to have any confusion about Frank's role in my life.

"Okay, PJ, where is your stepdad?" He had moved from the doorway into the room and was settling onto the couch opposite me. It was one of those fake brown leather couches that squishes air out of the cushions when you sit down. I kicked my backpack under my chair as I stood up and stepped toward the cafeteria door.

"Frank," I hollered, loud enough so he could hear me over the television. Every head turned toward me except his. "Frank," I called again. He pushed away from the table and turned toward me as he stood up. I pointed with my thumb over my shoulder toward the trooper.

Frank came in a direct line, pushing aside the chairs to his right and left as he bolted toward me. One even tipped over as it caught on a table leg. He left it on its side, kicking it farther back under the table with his foot as he swept by.

"You know what happened to Steph?" he asked as he brushed by me.

"Trooper Lawrence," the officer said as stood back up and offered his hand to Frank. I watched the cushion fill with air once more. He hadn't offered to shake my hand.

"Well, do you know?" Frank demanded as he shook the officer's hand.

"Not exactly. We're hoping to talk to her yet today. There seems to be some confusion about just what happened."

"Like what?" I asked.

"Well, she hit a telephone pole. We don't think she was going too fast, but it was fast enough to have done some serious damage to her car and for her to be pretty badly injured, as you know. A couple witnesses thought she swerved to avoid another car, but there is some disagreement on what the other car looked like and what it was doing."

"What kind of disagreement?" Frank asked.

"One person thought the other car was actually driving toward her, while another witness said there were two other cars in the area. Both agree, though, that there was a dark-colored car involved, black, or maybe blue, and that it was kind of sporty."

"Everybody knows everybody around here," Frank explained. "Nobody recognized who it was?"

"Apparently not," Trooper Lawrence explained. "One witness, who was coming out of the Midtown Market, doesn't live around here and was headed to Binghamton. The other was an older lady named, uh, let's see . . ." He flipped though the notebook he had in his left hand. "Jameson? Irma Jameson? That mean anything to you?"

Frank looked at me. He hadn't lived here all his life like I had.

"She isn't the lady who has her own shopping cart, is she, PJ?"

"Yup," I answered, turning my attention to the officer. "Everybody knows Old Lady Jameson is crazy. You can't believe anything she says."

"But she wanders up and down the sidewalk all the time," Frank interrupted, "and she really might have seen something."

"Or she might have just said she saw something," I continued. "Trust me, she's wacko."

"Well, her description of a car was similar to the other witness's description," Trooper Lawrence claimed. "And right now, that's all we have to go on. There was no evidence of another car hitting her: no paint, no lost part of another car, not even skid marks."

"How about her car? Where's that?" Frank asked.

"It's been towed to a garage." He looked at his notebook again. "Ernie's?" He looked up at Frank. "In fact, someone from the garage said you worked there."

Frank nodded. "Yeah, I do. How bad is her car?"

I wanted to punch him. Who cared about a stupid car?

"Well, she's not likely to drive it again. The front's bashed in, and considering how old it is, it's not likely to be worth fixing."

"Probably not," Frank agreed, nodding his head up and down, looking a little like a toy I had as a kid, a clown that popped out of a plastic box when you cranked out some tinny music. He had the same stupid look on his face, sort of like he was trying to smile and cry at the same time.

"You gonna find the person who ran her off the road?" I demanded. The car seemed the least of our concerns.

"Well, now, PJ, we don't know yet if she was forced off the road. That's why I need to talk to her. But we'll get to the bottom of this." He tapped his notebook with the finger of his right hand. "Was she feeling okay this morning? Upset about anything? Angry?"

"Huh?" I wondered if the last fifteen years counted.

"Upset? Angry? In a hurry? I need to know if just maybe she wasn't thinking clearly."

"Nah," Frank offered. "She was fine when I saw her this morning."

"That so, PJ?" I felt the officer's eyes piercing the top of my head while I examined my boots. He cleared his throat. "PJ?"

"Yeah, I guess she was fine." I pictured her sitting at the kitchen table, the pile of papers in front of her. "She was worried about the bills," I added. I didn't think her being annoyed at me meant anything. She was always annoyed at me.

"She's always worried about money," Frank added. "I don't think she ran off the road over that."

"Well, we have to check out all possibilities."

"Maybe you ought to start checking out that other car," Frank suggested. I was impressed by the insistence in his voice. The "cops are no good" biker Frank was back.

Chapter Seventeen

I woke up to the ringing of bells. That's the problem with living two blocks from a couple churches, especially two that start at the same time. They ought to have some consideration for those of us who don't go to church. Even my mom doesn't usually hassle me on Sundays, probably because that's the one day she gets to sleep late herself. Sometimes she works on Sunday, but not very often. Then again, maybe it's a good thing they all ring at the same time. It sort of gets all that dinging and donging out of the way.

I didn't really mind it the day after my mother's accident, though. I needed to be pushed out of bed. I took a shower and even put on clean clothes, at least clean underwear, socks, and a T-shirt. I hadn't worn my jeans all that much. They were good for another couple weeks. By the time I headed downstairs, I was feeling pretty good. Just starving.

Frank was nowhere to be found. I had figured he and I would head to the hospital together this morning. Instead, I found a note on the refrigerator when I got out the milk for my Cocoa Puffs, the only cereal in the cupboard and not my favorite breakfast food. Frank likes Cocoa Puffs. Sometimes he even eats them for supper when we're on our own.

See you at the hospital. Went to the shop first.

Great. Apparently Frank didn't care how I got to the hospital. Sure, I could walk there. But that wasn't the point. What was so important at Ernie's this morning that he had to go there? Probably to see the wreck. Ernie's wasn't open on Sundays. At least I didn't think so. By the time I usually got out of bed on a Sunday, Frank wasn't around, and I didn't care much where he was.

Ten minutes later, I dumped the empty bowl into the sink and headed out the door. Who knew how long Frank had been gone? He probably was at the hospital by now, and my mom was wondering where I was.

I was just about to cross Main Street when Mike Romano's blue Mustang pulled up along the curb.

"Hey there, Barnes. What's up?"

It was Kyle, with his head sticking ostrichlike out the car window, which was only down about halfway. I choked back a laugh.

"Need a ride?" he hollered just before his head popped back into the car and the door flew open. He leaned as far forward as he could, holding the back of the seat up against his side.

"C'mon, c'mon, get in."

Was this an offer or a command? Either way, it beat walking. Larry slid over behind Mike as I climbed into the back, dropping my backpack between us on the seat. My feet had hardly left the pavement when the door slammed and Mike took off.

Perhaps if Kyle's circle of friends had included better role models than the likes of Mike Romano or Larry Marston, he might have . . .

Mrs. Jordan's words bounced around in my head. So they weren't the best students in the world. I'm not so sure that made them criminals either. So they weren't known for their squeaky-clean behavior, and asking me to blackmail another student wasn't exactly going to get them the "good citizen of the week" award. But Mrs. Jordan didn't really know these guys at all. It's not like they were robbing banks or anything. She didn't really know them. Or anyone.

"Headin' to the hospital?" Mike asked.

"Yeah, in fact, I am," I answered, trying not to sound surprised that he knew. Which I was. "You heard about the accident, huh?"

"Everybody heard about the accident, Barnes," Larry replied. "Too bad about your old lady. She's gonna be okay, I hear."

"Yeah, she'll be fine." How much did they know? "So what did you guys hear about it?"

"Not much," Kyle offered, turning around in his seat so he could see me. "Heard she ran into a stop sign or something." He didn't sound particularly concerned.

"Telephone pole. She hit a telephone pole."

There was a long pause as we continued down Main Street. Kyle was facing the front again, and Larry began tapping the fingers of his right hand on his knee. Mike rolled down his window a little and flicked his cigarette out into the street. He reached up and twisted the rearview mirror, where our eyes met just as he began to speak.

"Okay, Barnes, you thought about our offer? Seems to me you could use the money. What with your mom laid up an' all. In fact, we got some other possibilities for you. What d'ya think? Can we count on you?"

"I dunno," I mumbled as I looked away from the mirror.

Kyle let out a slow whistle from the front seat. "C'mon, PJ, what's the big deal? You just pass on a message. What's so hard about that? Big Shot Brian Carson has become your newfound friend or something?"

"I just haven't thought about it, that's all." I tried not to sound hostile, but I could hear the anger in my voice. What did they think I had been doing for twenty-four hours? Weighing the pros and cons of their offer?

Mike pulled into the parking lot of the hospital and did a U-turn so he was facing the exit. Kyle flung open the door and hopped out, pulling the seat forward as he did. As I stepped out onto the pavement, he grabbed my left arm and held me back.

"Don't let us down, Barnes. You gotta make a choice. You're with us or you're against us. It's pretty simple."

Nothing was that simple. I jerked my arm away and flung my backpack over my shoulder as I turned to face him.

"I'll let you know tomorrow."

Kyle glared back at me and hopped back into the Mustang. I watched as Mike peeled out of the driveway, turning left, the sporty, dark blue car speeding back toward the center of town. I felt a knot tighten in my stomach.

Chapter Eighteen

"You couldn't wait for me?" I whispered harshly to Frank as I entered my mom's room. Her eyes were closed, and I assumed she was asleep.

"You were still in bed," he answered loudly. "I had things to do. I left you a note."

"For cryin' out loud, Frank," I hissed again. "Don't you think you could be a little quieter."

"It's okay, PJ. I'm awake," my mother answered weakly, her eyes still closed.

"See? You woke her up."

"She's been awake, PJ." He spoke slowly and calmly. "They just gave her something for the pain, though, and she's getting a little sleepy again."

I was angry, but Frank wasn't taking the bait. Like I said, he wasn't very good at arguing. He was more likely to just wander away and look for a television set.

"Don't argue, you two."

"Sorry, Mom." I was. There I was, finally able to talk to her for the first time since yesterday morning, and what did I do but screw everything up.

"Frank, I want to talk to PJ alone."

I had to give Frank credit. I would have been pissed if she had told me to leave the room. Not Frank. He patted her on the hand and left the room without a word.

"You okay, PJ?" Her voice was raspy, as though she needed a drink of water. She opened her eyes and tried to smile, but it seemed forced. Her lips were too evenly spread apart, and her eyebrows were scrunched together over her nose. I couldn't tell if she was having a hard time seeing me or if she was still in pain. As I came closer to the side of her bed, she lifted her right hand and reached out toward me. I took it and noticed how cold it was.

Her question was ridiculous. She was the one in bed, in pain. And then I remembered how I'd asked Frank the day before if he was okay. Maybe it did make sense.

"Okay," I answered, probably too quietly for her to hear. I wanted to say I was sorry, sorry that I had been so miserable yesterday morning. I wanted to shout out that I was a jerk and that I would try not to screw up so much. I wanted to tell her that I had been scared that she was going to die.

"I'm okay," I repeated, this time louder, more self-confident. I wanted her to think she could count on me. She didn't need me to worry about right now. After all, she had Frank. That was enough.

"I want to talk to you about Frank," she began.

"What about Frank?" I asked.

"I just need to know that you two will be okay. I have a feeling I'm not going home for a couple days."

A couple days? What an understatement. My mother had more tubes coming out of her than Mr. Cavanaugh's strangest lab project.

"Probably more than just a couple, Mom." She ignored me.

"You're going to have to take care of him, PJ. We both know he's not very responsible."

Here was my mother, talking to me like we were the parents and Frank was the child. I wasn't so sure I wanted the responsibility. Or maybe she was using that perverse psychology on me, getting me to think I was the important one. I wondered if she had used the same line on Frank. Sort of . . . "Take care of PJ, Frank. He's going through a hard time right now."

"Frank'll be okay." I watched him fold temporarily yesterday and rebound after a session with some coffee and TV. "He will."

"Promise me you won't fight."

"We don't fight." It was true. Maybe there was an occasional snide remark on my part, but Frank rarely responded. Mostly we'd had lots of experience ignoring each other.

"Promise me," she insisted.

"I promise. I promise." Parents are always asking you to promise them something, aren't they?

Her shoulders settled back into the pillow.

"Thanks, sweetie." She hadn't called me sweetie in years, probably not since Frank came on the scene. "And . . . PJ?"

"Yeah?"

"I'm sorry about the working papers. I'll sign them, or Frank can. He will. I told him it was okay."

"Thanks, Mom."

"And try to keep your schoolwork up."

Okay, okay. So much for feeling like the responsible one. I was still getting lectured.

"Promise me you'll try," she insisted.

See? Promises.

"I'll try. I'll try," I answered, trying not to sound annoyed.

She squeezed my hand and closed her eyes again.

"You want me to stay for a while? Or maybe I should go so you can rest." Part of me wanted stay, but most of me wanted to leave.

"Promise me you'll come back later," she insisted, her eyes still closed.

There was an awful lot of promising going on.

Chapter Nineteen

Frank was in the lounge, already drinking coffee. I wondered where he'd found money since yesterday. Maybe he did know about the jar in the cupboard. He looked up as I entered.

"She asleep?"

"Yeah, I think so."

"I'm goin' back down to Ernie's. You want a lift home?"

What was with this guy? Didn't he think he should stay?

"No, I'm gonna stay." I expected him to take the hint.

"She'll probably sleep for most of the day. You just gonna hang out here?"

"For a while. I'll go back down to her room later."

"Suit yourself." He slugged down the last of his coffee and tossed the empty cup into the wastebasket next to the door.

"So what's goin' on at Ernie's on a Sunday, Frank? Checkin'

out Mom's wrecked car?" I asked as he headed out the door. The promise to my mother was fading fast. I didn't even try to hide the sarcasm.

Frank stopped abruptly and turned slightly, those steely blue eyes staring right at me. He looked terrible. He needed a shave badly, his straggly hair hung limp around his face, and he had the same clothes on that he did yesterday. He wasn't the neatest man in town, but he was always pretty clean, especially for a guy who worked on cars all the time, and although it was often hard to tell if he was intending to grow a beard or not, his long hair was usually tied back in a ponytail.

"Work, PJ," he answered calmly. "Ernie said I could work as many hours as I wanted, whenever I wanted. It'll be a while before your mom is back to work." He turned and left.

Just great. PJ the jerk. I flung my backpack across the room onto the couch and threw myself into the nearest chair.

"Frank!" I hollered as I jumped up from the chair. "Frank!" I called, racing down the hall after him.

"Shh," a nurse scolded as I swept by her.

I reached the reception area just as Frank disappeared out the exit.

"Frank!" I hollered again.

"PJ Barnes, lower your voice," the woman at the reception desk insisted.

"I gotta talk to Frank," I explained as I pushed through the exit doors. He had stopped just outside.

"What?" he asked.

"My working papers. Mom said you could sign them."

He nodded. "Okay, where are they?"

They were in my backpack back in the lounge.

"Wait here. I'll get them."

I ran back through the reception area and down the hall into the lounge again. The same nurse who shushed me scowled as I sped by her.

I dumped the contents of my pack onto the couch. The papers were in there somewhere. I'd almost thrown them away the other night when my mom was being a pill about the whole thing. There they were, sticking out from underneath Henry's copy of *Rolling Stone*. I headed back to the exit and then turned and grabbed a pen.

When I got back to the reception area, Frank was inside waiting for me. He took the papers and pen, squatted down beside an end table, and scrawled his name in the two places marked with an X. He handed them back to me, tucked the pen in his shirt pocket, and left without a word.

Part of me wished I had let Frank take me home. Sitting around the waiting room wasn't going to be much fun. I wandered back to the lounge, glad I'd grabbed a handful of change from the jar in the cupboard before I left so I could get a soda or something. I'd thought about going back to my mom's room, where I could just wait for her to wake up again so I could say good-bye and get out of there. We didn't have much to talk about. But there wasn't really any place to sit in her room, and Frank was probably right about her sleeping for quite a while.

When I got back to the lounge, I tucked the working papers into an outer pocket of my backpack and began straightening up the mess I'd left on the couch. Homework papers for English were spread all over, a glaring reminder of the promise to my mother. I really had tried to think about homework the past two days, and I had done some. That should count for something. I meant what I told her about trying. At least I meant it when I said it. But, frankly, I really couldn't imagine doing it all. I had my English homework in my pack because Mrs. Jordan made me take it. Who knew whether or not I had homework in any other subject. This promise was not going to be easy.

I picked up the copy of *Rolling Stone* and set it on the end table next to the couch. That was one thing I didn't mind reading over and over. I stacked up the rest of the stuff, planning to slide it into the bottom of my pack, when Mrs. Jordan's journal slid onto the floor. A bottom corner had bent upward, and I felt a knot growing in my stomach. It was like she was following my every move, spying on me, just waiting for me to screw up. I picked it up and folded the corner back down. Maybe it would flatten out if I put a book down on top of it. I had told myself I was returning it on Monday. Maybe I should have just thrown it away.

I didn't. Instead, I sat down and opened it up and started skimming through it again, looking to see what else she had written about me. There it was.

When PJ Barnes came into class today and muttered "F— you" under his breath as he slammed his books down on the desk . . .

What was she talking about? I didn't remember that happening. I glanced back at the entry before it. Mrs. Jordan should date her stuff. Sometimes she did, but mostly not. She just wrote one thing and then skipped a little space and wrote some more. If I did that on an essay, she'd make me do it over. That is, if I did my essays.

I tapped my name on the page. Boy, did I sound like a loser.

She made it sound like we fought a lot, which we didn't. I mean, she and I didn't see eye to eye on things like doing homework and paying attention in class, but I don't remember slamming my books down. Maybe it was the day I saw Heather and Nicko with their bodies wrapped around each other. Minds in tune? Yeah, right.

When will PJ learn that everyone is not his enemy . . .

Everyone isn't?

. . . that the world is not his enemy. The only enemy PJ has stares back at him every day in the mirror . . . so alone . . . anger and hostility . . . a lack of love and attention . . .

I sat with the blue notebook opened in my hands for what seemed like hours, sinking deeper into the couch, staring at the opposite wall. How could she think this about me? My cheeks grew hot. I was embarrassed. I sounded pathetic.

Is that really how she saw me? Lonely, disturbed, angry, ready to go over the edge? She didn't know me at all. She obviously didn't know about Heather. Okay, so maybe I was a little miserable sometimes, maybe a little weird. But I wasn't about to bomb the school or run through the halls with a weapon. She thought I lacked attention? I got more than I needed or wanted. A little less would have been just fine with me.

She's got everybody labeled, and I just don't fit. I'm not a jock or a nerd or a prep. Sure, I play soccer, but I'm not very good. And I entered a science contest in middle school, but I didn't win anything, even though Mrs. Dunkirk said it was the best explanation of electricity she'd ever seen. And being a prep is impossible. After all, I live with my mom and Frank. Wal-Mart gets our business, not L.L. Bean. So alone? I've always moved sort of on the fringe. But

I've got friends! At least Henry and Billy . . . I think. And I had a girlfriend . . . once. So what if I don't belong to any *group*? What business is it of hers?

"Hey, PJ, how ya doin'?"

The voice startled me, and when I looked up, there stood Billy, leaning on his crutches, and Henry, standing behind him in the doorway.

"Hey, guys." I closed the notebook, being careful to cover the right-hand corner with the fingers of my left hand so Mrs. Jordan's name, which seemed to be flashing in neon lights, could not be seen, and nonchalantly slid it down into the side of my backpack.

Henry edged his way around Billy and settled in the chair next to the door. "How's your mom?"

"Okay, I think. She's sleeping right now."

"Billy called last night and told me," Henry continued. "We thought maybe you'd want some company." He looked around the tiny room and leaned forward a little to peer into the cafeteria. "Your dad's not here?"

The guys referred to Frank as my dad, even though they knew he wasn't my real dad. I guess it just made it easier. In fact, I don't think they'd ever met my real dad. They hadn't missed anything.

"No, he had to go to work."

"He tell you I called last night?" Billy asked as he hobbled toward the couch.

"You called?"

"Sure," Billy emphasized. "My mom told me about your mom when she got home. It was pretty late when I called, though. Your dad said you'd already gone to bed. I told him to let you know Henry and I would see you today."

"Frank didn't say anything," I explained. "He probably just forgot." Why make excuses for Frank? Of course Frank forgot.

"We called your house this morning, but nobody was there," Henry added.

"So, how's she doin'?" Billy asked.

I slid over as Billy eased himself onto the couch, keeping his left leg as level as possible, his right leg bent at the knee with his foot pressed firmly on the floor.

"Hard to tell," I told him. ". . . but okay. Nothing that won't heal . . . eventually."

"You know how it happened?" Billy continued. "My mom said no one really knew."

"Nope. Not yet," I told him. "She doesn't remember much."

Henry was leaning forward in his chair, his elbows on his knees, his hands folded in front of him. We sat in silence for a couple minutes. I was glad they were there. It was pretty neat that they'd come down to see me and all, but there isn't a lot to say when you're just waiting.

"So," Henry asked, looking around the lounge, "what do you do while you wait in a place like this?"

"Just wait, mostly. Do a little homework," I said as I pointed my foot toward my backpack, which was now sitting on the floor underneath Billy's left foot.

"Read a good magazine," I added, waving my hand at Henry's copy of *Rolling Stone*.

"You doin' homework?" Billy asked in disbelief.

"Yeah," I answered. "Tryin'."

"The new you, huh? Model student?" Henry laughed as he leaned forward and shook his finger at me. "I guess it beats stayin' after school all the time."

In spite of Henry's recent contract with his father, he was hardly a model student. His comment was a little unfair.

"Just some English," I offered as explanation. "No big deal. It's almost done."

"Uh-huh. Yeah, sure, PJ," Henry said. I hoped he wasn't going to ask for proof.

More silence. There wasn't much to say about homework.

"You guys want something from the cafeteria?" I nodded toward the open doorway, hoping neither one took me up on the offer. The handful of change I had in my pocket wouldn't go far.

"Nah," Billy answered. "I'm still full of pancakes." He began tapping the end of one of his crutches on the floor. He looked bored.

"Me, too," Henry answered. "Billy's mom makes the best pancakes."

I don't think my mom knows how to make pancakes.

More silence.

"Hey, guys. Look, it was really great of you to come down here. I mean, I really appreciate it. I'll tell my mom when she wakes up. She'll like that." I was hoping they would take the hint. "In fact, I probably ought to check on her soon to see if she's awake."

Billy came to my rescue.

"We gotta go anyway. My mom was stopping back for us after she took Grandma home. She said to tell your mom she'd see her tomorrow," he explained.

"Hope she's okay," Henry added as he rose to his feet. "You sure we can't do anything for you?"

"Nah, I'm fine. I got nothin' better to do than wait."

Billy pulled himself to his feet and swung the end of one of his crutches against the side of my leg. "Hang in there, PJ. She'll be fine."

I felt miserable. I didn't want them to stay. But I was still glad they had shown up. Mrs. Jordan was wrong. I had friends. I had thought maybe I would tell them about the journal, that they'd get a kick out of it or help me figure out what to do about it. Not anymore.

"Hey, guys?" I turned sideways in my chair.

Henry was already in the hall, but Billy was still only halfway through the door. He stopped and pivoted on his one good leg so that our eyes met.

"You think I'm a loser?"

Billy didn't smile or make some wisecrack. I was glad. I wasn't trying to be funny. He raised his eyebrows, almost as though he was looking into the air for an answer, and then he tipped his head slightly to one side like he was really thinking about my question. After a long four or five seconds, he straightened his head and looked directly into my eyes.

"If you're a loser, PJ, then you got lots of company."

Chapter Twenty

"You wanta be a loser all your life, Barnes?" Kyle Hawkins whispered to me as he slid into the desk next to me.

Kyle had been waiting at my locker just before the first bell rang and stuck like glue all the way to English class. I tried to ignore him. I couldn't be late. Not today. Mrs. Jordan might think I was desperate for attention, but I wasn't going to give her any more reason to make me her target.

"You've had time to think," he'd hissed in my ear as he slipped past me into the room just as the bell rang.

What I didn't want was time to think. I had too much to think about.

"Good morning, everyone." Mrs. Jordan closed the door and began handing out blue sheets. Monday. Vocabulary day. She was already on a roll. "Let's go over the words for pronunciation and parts of speech."

Just like a robot, all mechanical . . . no blood, no guts, no heart.

"But, first, I want to ask again if anyone has seen my missing notebook."

She was worried. Good. Serves her right. Writing all that stuff about people. I should have thrown it away.

"Has anyone?"

Yeah, sure, Mrs. Jordan. Here it is. Right here, tucked away in the bottom of my backpack.

Silence. A couple kids shrugged.

"You thought about a reward yet?" Kyle was leaning forward as far as he could in his seat, as though he were waiting eagerly for an answer. "I know some people who could use the money." He grinned in my direction. I felt my face grow hot as I reached for the blue paper Tracy Johnston was waving over her shoulder in front of me.

"Do these 'some people' know where my notebook is, Kyle?" Mrs. Jordan asked, peering over the edge of her glasses.

Kyle shrugged and sat back in his desk.

"Beats me. I was just asking."

I stared at the blue sheet on my desk. *Shut up, Kyle.*

"Some people don't do things just for money, Kyle."

"No kidding? That so, Mrs. Jordan? I don't know any"—he paused and made a big show of pointing to the first word on the sheet—"'altruistic' people."

The class laughed.

"Okay, Kyle, you've made your point. Time for vocabulary."

The class groaned. Watching Kyle and Mrs. Jordan spar was much more interesting than doing schoolwork.

"PJ? Since Kyle was kind of enough to give the pronunciation—correctly I might add, Kyle—maybe you could tell us the part of speech."

Of course Kyle could pronounce it correctly. He'd already taken this class once before.

"PJ?"

"I don't know."

"I suspect you do. Just think about it. Kyle said he didn't know any altruistic people. It describes the type of people. What type of words describe nouns?"

I hated it when she did that. Said kids knew stuff when they clearly didn't. Who cares about parts of speech? My mother was in the hospital, I was being asked to blackmail the school bully, and everyone thinks I'm a loser.

"I said I don't know. Leave me alone," I yelled loudly.

The classroom went silent. Nobody said a word. Not even Kyle. I felt stupid. I *was* a loser.

"Okay, PJ, I hear you," Mrs. Jordan said after what seemed like a lifetime of silence. She paused for just a moment and then continued as though I wasn't even there. "Danette, part of speech?"

I zoned out for the rest of class, and the next thing I knew the ending bell was ringing. Kyle muttered under his breath to me as he got up from his seat.

"Way to go, Barnes," he whispered sarcastically.

"C'mon, PJ. Let's go." It was Henry, standing in front of my desk. I'd made no effort to move. Everyone else was already at the door, pushing their way into the hall.

"PJ," Mrs. Jordan called from the front of the room, where she was dropping some papers into the recycling box. "Stay for a moment, please. I'll give you a pass if you're late."

Henry looked at me as though I had just been sentenced to prison or run over by a truck or told I had a month to live. His concern made me feel pretty good.

"You go on to class, Henry," she commanded.

"Okay," Henry answered quietly. He probably figured I was doomed.

"And close the door, please," she added as he was leaving.

When the door was closed, she turned her attention to me. I braced myself, waiting for the lecture. Let's see, would it be one or two days of detention?

"How's your mom?"

"My mom?"

"Yes, PJ, your mom. I heard about the accident."

"She'll be in the hospital for a while, but she's doing okay," I answered cautiously. What was she up to?

"You let me know when she's able to have some company. I'd like to stop in to see her."

I almost fell out of my seat. I didn't think she was talking about a parent-teacher conference here. I think she really meant she would stop in and just see my mom, like a regular person would. I don't think it had anything to do with me.

"You know, PJ, your mom was one of my students, too."

Stephanie Blake was a rather sweet thing, though always looking somewhat forlorn as though she was in desperate need of some attention, some affection.

"Yeah, I know," I answered before I realized what I was saying.

"Oh, you do?"

Think quickly. Was this a trick? Maybe she really didn't care about my mother at all. Maybe she was just trying to see if I had her journal, if I had read it. I wanted to look at her face, to see if I could tell what she was thinking. But I didn't dare. I just stared at the top of the desk.

"Yeah, uh, I think she mentioned it, maybe during the summer or something." I sounded stupid. Was Mrs. Jordan really going to believe that my mom and I spent the summer talking about school and teachers?

She didn't say anything for a long time. I didn't know whether to go on to my next class or not. Pretty soon I heard her rummaging around at her desk. When I looked up, she was writing out a pass.

"You let me know when she feels like having visitors, okay?" she asked as she handed me the pass.

"Yeah," I answered as I took the pass and headed for the door. I just wanted to be out of there.

"And, PJ?" Her voice was quiet, but it had that "I'm in charge" tone. "No more outbursts."

I didn't turn around. I didn't look at her. But I could feel her eyes staring at me as I nodded. I opened the door and escaped into the hall.

The day had started badly, and I spent the rest of it avoiding people. During lunch I sat at one of the carrels in the back of the library. It was the last place Kyle or Larry or Mike would think to look for me. I needed time to think. Which I might have done if the librarian hadn't kept swooping by every few minutes, asking if I needed any help with anything. I think she thought I was a new student.

Henry raised his eyebrows at me in biology when I came in, but Mr. Cavanaugh had already started explaining the lab project. I hadn't seen him since English, and he probably thought I was in trouble with Mrs. Jordan. I shook my head no and took my seat near the back. After class, he left quickly, and I didn't see him for the rest of the day. I figured he was busy helping Billy carry his stuff around.

I even managed to get to the end of the day before I saw Brian Carson at all. And that was only from a distance as I was leaving the building. He was turning the corner, heading down the hall to the gym wing. I wasn't going to soccer practice. In fact, I was quitting the team. Brian wasn't going to care whether I did or not, so it probably didn't matter whether I saw him or not. But it did to Mike Romano.

"Hey, Barnes, where ya goin'?" It was Mike, standing beside his Mustang in the faculty section of the parking lot. "Don't you have practice?"

"I'm quitting. I'm getting a job." I continued on down the sidewalk. I didn't owe him any explanation.

"Whoa, there, Barnes. You *got* a job. Remember?" I heard the door slam shut. He jogged around the front of his car and moved in step beside me. "You and I have a deal." He put his hand on my forearm and pulled me back slightly.

I stopped abruptly and wheeled around to face him.

"Get your hands off me. We do not have a deal."

His lock on my arm grew tighter. He's only a few inches taller than I am, but he outweighs me by at least thirty pounds. I wasn't going anywhere.

"We need to have a little talk, Barnes. I thought we had an understanding."

"I said I'd think about it."

I had thought about it. It was too complicated. Brian Carson was not going to worry about anything I might say to Coach. He'd figure Lockwood would think I was totally unreliable, especially quitting the team with only a few games left. And I was getting a job. I couldn't get the job and still play soccer.

"What's to think about? What kind of a job will pay you forty bucks for a conversation?"

He did have a point.

"Well, Barnes? What job are you talking about?"

What the hell. Maybe if he realized I was serious, he'd get off my case.

"Midtown Market."

He let go of my arm and laughed. Not mean. Just like he'd heard something really funny.

"You got a job at Midtown Market? You sure about that?"

"Yeah, I do. What's the joke?"

He ignored the question.

"You want a ride to your new job?" Now his tone *was* sarcastic.

"I'll walk."

"Suit yourself," he hollered as he backed away, shaking his head. "My offer still stands. You let me know when you're ready to collect."

He hopped into his Mustang and started the engine. He revved it several times before he backed up and swung toward the exit. As he sped by me, he tooted the horn. I looked up just in time to see a long deep scratch on the back fender. It was several seconds before I began breathing again.

Chapter Twenty-one

"But I don't understand. You said I just needed to get my working papers. They're all set." They were. I'd left them in the high school office that morning.

"Sorry. You didn't come back on Friday," Mr. Prindle explained as he continued bagging groceries. "I assumed you weren't interested. It's too late now. I hired somebody else on Saturday."

"But you said I could have the job."

"Look, kid, I told you to get your working papers straightened out and then come back. You didn't come back. I hired someone else. If he doesn't work out, you can have the job if you're still interested. Besides, it was only a few hours after school and some Saturdays." He tossed a loaf of bread in a bag and handed it to some old lady I didn't recognize.

"Who took my job?" I demanded.

"It wasn't your job," he answered. He shook open a fresh paper bag and balanced it on the counter, waiting for the cashier to begin checking out the next customer. "But it was Larry Marston," he continued, "not that it should matter."

"Larry Marston?" I blurted the name out so loudly the cashier jerked her head around to look at me. Larry Marston took a job? Took *my* job?

"Yes," Prindle answered sharply. "Look, kid, I've got a business to run here. I'm sorry about the job, but you're a little younger than I wanted anyway."

"I gotta ask you something."

He sighed and leaned on the counter with both of his hands flat in front of him.

"What?"

"Did Larry know I was asking for that job?"

He looked at me kind of funny, pushed his eyebrows together like he was thinking, and then shook his head back and forth.

"I don't think so," he answered. "I don't remember your name coming up. He came in, said he heard I had a job opening, and wanted to know if it was still available. That was it."

"And that was Saturday?"

"Yeah, Saturday." He began dropping cans into the bag. "Check back in a few weeks. Maybe something will open up."

"Yeah, sure," I snarled as I flung my backpack over my shoulder and headed toward the exit. This was smalltown. No fancy electronic doors here. I pushed on the metal bar as hard as I could. The door flung wide open, hitting the brick wall of the entryway. I stepped into the afternoon sunshine.

There in the parking lot, waiting to greet me, oozing victory, was Mike Romano, sitting on the hood of his car, and Kyle Hawkins, leaning against the front left fender.

"You bastard," I shouted as I dropped my backpack and flew toward the front of the Mustang, my fists ready.

"Easy there, Barnes," Mike said as he hopped off the hood and held his arms straight out to stop my advance. "Grab him, Kyle."

Kyle swooped around behind me and quickly had a tight hold on both my arms.

"You knew, you sonofabitch. You knew Larry had my job."

"I didn't know it was your job, Barnes, not until this afternoon. It was too perfect. Too perfect." He settled back against the front of his car.

"Let go of me," I yelled.

"No way, PJ."

"You had to know. He took the job just so I wouldn't, didn't he? You had it all planned." I kicked at the pavement, sending a spray of gravel into the side of his car.

"Hey, kid! You leave my car out of this." His tone had become angry. "Do not mess with my property. You hear?"

He couldn't have been any angrier than I was. My face grew hot and my eyes began to burn. I squirmed under Kyle's grip and tried using my butt to throw him off balance.

"Was my mom's accident part of this plan, too? Or was that just a great coincidence for you?"

Kyle's grip on my arms eased for a moment, and I almost escaped, but his fingers instantly pressed into my upper arms, holding me in place even tighter.

"What're you talkin' about?" He sounded confused.

"That." I nodded with my head toward the side of the Mustang. Mike stepped away from the hood and turned to look down the side of his car.

"What about it?" he asked as he turned his head to look back at me.

I glared at him.

"You do that Saturday?"

"As a matter of fact, I did." He reached down with his right hand and drew his fingers lightly over the scratch. "Too close to a mailbox. Not a big deal. I'll get it fixed."

"Right." I wasn't buying his story.

"It's true, PJ. I was with him," Kyle offered as he turned me around to face him, releasing his hold on me. "Out on River Road."

Romano was scum. Kyle was, too. But his explanation sounded sincere, and his face showed no guilt. I turned my attention back to Mike.

"You telling me you didn't run my mother off the road?"

"I'm telling you I don't know what you're talkin' about."

"You weren't here Saturday afternoon with Larry, taking my job away?"

"For chrissakes, will you get off this job bit." He reached forward and grabbed my left arm, pulling me toward him. His face was inches from mine. Kyle grabbed my right arm and twisted it up behind me.

"Larry took a job here because it suits our plans. You understand? It has nothin' to do with you. And he isn't going to keep it for very long, so if you really want this *j-o-b*, you can have it pretty soon. That is, if you think that jerk in there will give it to you after you left pouting like a little brat."

He had a point. I felt the tension go out of my body, and Mike and Kyle must have, too, because they let go of me at just about the same time. I was still angry, but I felt more like crying than fighting. I just didn't know what to do.

"C'mon, Barnes, get in the car," Mike commanded, but neither he nor Kyle laid a hand on me. "Get in the front."

Kyle grabbed my pack and threw it into the backseat, pulling the front seat back as he slid in next to it. I climbed into the front and slammed the door shut.

"Where're we goin'?" I demanded as Mike wheeled out of the parking lot.

"Soccer practice."

"What?" I snapped. The anger returned.

"Soccer practice," Mike repeated calmly. "You tell anybody you were quitting?"

"No," I answered quietly. I hadn't. I figured I just wouldn't show up.

"You don't have a real job," Mike reminded me. "Remember? Larry didn't take your job away. Prindle gave it away. So it seems to me that our deal ought to look pretty good. Doesn't it?"

My head was spinning. This didn't make any sense. Lockwood would be pissed that I showed up an hour late for practice. How was that going to help my so-called credibility?

"You're crazy," I muttered. I was beginning to think that was the truth.

"Well, Barnes, you are not the first person to think that," Mike answered with a laugh.

Chapter Twenty-two

"I can't believe you don't have to run a zillion laps today," Henry shouted as he huffed and puffed his way up beside me.

"I think he felt sorry for me," I explained. When Mike dropped me off at soccer practice the day before, the first thing Coach Lockwood asked about was my mother. Everybody knew about her accident.

"And Billy said he didn't even yell," he continued.

"He didn't even ask why I was late," I boasted. "I think he figured I was at the hospital."

"Were you?"

Henry's question had a guarded tone to it, like he knew I wasn't.

"No," I answered, slowing down to a jog. I hadn't run a zillion laps, but I was still exhausted. Henry slowed his pace to mine.

"I didn't think so."

"Oh yeah? Why not?"

"Billy saw you getting out of Mike Romano's car."

"What makes you think he didn't give me a ride from the hospital?"

"Did he?"

"No." There was no reason to lie to Henry. "What was Billy doing at practice anyway?" Henry had already told me why *he* hadn't been there. Dentist appointment. Henry had great teeth.

"Just watching. Coach told him he needed him to analyze the plays, that he could be sort of an objective presence. I think he feels bad that Billy got hurt."

That was the second time in a week I'd heard Henry use the phrase *objective presence*. Did Lockwood really say that? Probably not. More likely it's lawyer talk. Was Henry becoming more and more like his dad?

"What're you doing with Romano and his creeps?"

That was unusually blunt for Henry. I wondered if he was still sore because I took a ride home with Mike last week. I stopped jogging and put my hands on my knees to catch my breath.

"They're not so bad," I offered as an explanation. I mostly wanted to convince myself that they weren't. They hadn't done anything to hurt me, not really. They had offered me a chance to make a few bucks. And at least they were up front with me. They weren't pretending to be my friends. It was just business.

"They're low-life, PJ. And they're trouble."

"What do you care?" I snapped, still staring at the ground. Henry didn't say a word. When I looked up, he was halfway around the field.

It was a stupid thing to say. He hadn't done anything to me.

By the time I got back to the bench, most of the team had already taken off. A couple guys were hopping into Brian Carson's Jeep, and two or three teammates had already started across the field toward town. Lockwood was tossing equipment into the trunk of his car, and Henry was stuffing his shin guards into his backpack.

"You guys all set here?" Lockwood hollered as he slammed the trunk down.

"Yeah, Coach," Henry hollered back. "All set."

"You, too, Barnes?"

"Yeah, I'm fine," I huffed as I walked around in a couple short circles, trying to catch my breath. I wasn't big on cooling down. The walk home took care of that.

"See you guys tomorrow then. Short practice. Game Thursday." He hopped into his car, an ancient black Ford Taurus, and started the engine. It coughed one or twice and then took hold as he revved the motor. A fog of blue smoke filled the air as he drove off the field onto the side road that bordered the soccer field.

"You got any water, PJ?"

Apparently I had already been forgiven. The guy was willing to share my water.

"Yeah, front pocket." I scooped up my shin guards and sweatshirt from underneath the bench where I had kicked them before running laps. Henry grabbed my backpack and unzipped the top.

"There's no water in here, butthead." He had pulled up some stuff from inside the center section of my pack. A corner of Mrs. Jordan's journal glared at me.

"Front pocket," I yelled as I grabbed the backpack away. "You got no ears? Front pocket."

"Whoa there, PJ." He jumped back and threw his hands into the air. "You got a bomb in there or something? A million bucks you stole from the lunch ladies in the cafeteria? A little stash of hash or something?" His tone moved quickly from teasing to sarcasm.

"Knock it off, Rose." I never called Henry by his last name. He knew I was pissed.

"No problemo, Barnes. I guess I'm not that thirsty." He flung his backpack over his shoulder and stalked off the field.

"Henry," I called after him. He threw his right hand into the air and twisted his fingers into a wave. He never looked back.

"Screw you," I muttered as I threw my pack over my shoulder and headed home. So much for friends.

I was almost to the end of School Street when Lockwood's vehicular disaster pulled up beside me along the curb on the wrong side of the road.

"You need a ride, PJ?"

His voice startled me, and his question took me by surprise. First of all, he never called me PJ during practice or a game. I guess we had officially gone beyond practice time. And second, he had never offered me a ride home before, or anyone else as far as I knew. I hesitated, searching for a response. Can you say no to your coach? What if someone saw me with him? Henry thought I was a jerk as it was. Would he think I was sucking up to the coach, taking advantage of him because he probably felt sorry for me with my mom in the hospital? I glanced down the street. Henry was nowhere to be seen. Why not?

"Yeah, thanks, Coach." I jogged around to the passenger side of his car and started to open the door when a car turned the corner in front of us, heading back up toward the school. I leaned against the side of the car as a black Jeep Wrangler passed by. It was Brian Carson. We exchanged glances briefly as he sped by. I wondered if my face showed as much surprise as his did.

"So, home or to the hospital?" Lockwood asked as I closed the car door.

"Hospital, I guess." My plan had been to go home, grab something to eat, and then head to the hospital later. My mom wasn't going anywhere. I'm not sure why I changed my mind. Maybe I wanted Coach to think I was being a good son or something.

"How's your mom doing?"

"Okay. She's pretty banged up. But she's gonna be okay."

"I'm glad to hear that. I knew your mom in high school. Bet you didn't know that."

I wasn't quite sure how I was supposed to answer. No, I didn't know that.

"Well, sort of, I guess," he continued. "She was in some of my classes when we were in junior high. Pretty, but shy. I must admit I don't remember her too much in high school."

Barry ... high school hero ... homecoming king ... super-athlete ... is he trying to relive the past through his students? ...

Maybe because you were somebody and she wasn't, I wanted to shout in his face. *Maybe because she quit. You don't remember the pregnant girl who quit school?* ... somewhat of a lost soul, like PJ ... *Did everyone think I was a loser? That my parents were losers?*

"Well, I'm glad she's going to be okay," he added. "I had an accident once and, let me tell you, that recovery was not . . ."

I tuned him out. I wasn't interested in his accident or his recovery. I was beginning to wish I hadn't accepted his offer of a ride. From now on, I was walking everywhere. No rides with anyone.

"Here you go, bud." He had pulled up to the emergency entrance. "Tell your mom I said hello."

I wanted to tell him to tell her himself. She could use a few visitors. As far as I knew, Frank and I were the only ones besides the people she worked with at the hospital who had been to see her. But what was the point?

"Thanks for the ride, Coach," I mumbled as I hopped out onto the pavement. I had never gone into the hospital through the emergency doors. I wondered if it was okay. I watched Lockwood drive away and then walked around to the side entrance.

When I entered my mom's room, she was sitting up in bed, eating supper. It didn't look like much, just some soup, but it was the first I'd seen her eating anything since Saturday. "Well, I didn't expect to see you until later."

"Coach gave me a ride," I offered as though that explained everything.

"You had any supper yet?"

I shook my head no.

"Want some of this?" She scooped up a spoonful of thin brown stuff and let it pour off her spoon back into the bowl.

"I'll pass."

"I thought so. Me, too." She laid the spoon onto the tray and pushed the narrow table away from her.

"Don't you think you ought to eat it?"

"Oh, they put enough stuff into you here with this." She

146

lifted her arm that had the IV in it. "They just give people real food—well, sort of real food—to make us think we're getting better. I know all the tricks."

I laughed. We were having a conversation, a real conversation, maybe the first conversation we had ever had.

"Frank told me about the job. I'm sorry, PJ."

I shrugged my shoulders. I hadn't told her the night before. It hadn't seemed necessary. I wouldn't have told Frank if he hadn't asked. I was surprised he did. Of course I figured he was just hoping there'd be some extra money.

"Maybe it's for the best," she added.

"Yeah, sure." I didn't know what else to say.

"It's not like you'd been looking for a job for a long time or anything."

"Drop it, Mom. It doesn't matter."

She looked at me like I had thrown the soup in her face. I might just as well have. So much for the real conversation.

"So Barry Lockwood dropped you off, huh?"

I guess she was trying to change the subject. I was surprised she knew who my coach was. Most of the time, she didn't even remember what sport I played, much less who was coaching.

"Yeah. He said to say hi, said he hoped you were doing better."

"That was nice of him."

"Yeah, I guess so. He also said he knew you in high school."

"He did? No kidding?" She reached up and pushed some hair away from her forehead and looked up toward the ceiling, like she was picturing something far away. "I'm surprised Barry Lockwood knew I was alive. Big shot and all in high school that he was."

"Well, he says he did."

"No kidding?"

The conversation was getting boring, and I was starved. It was time to make a diplomatic exit.

"Well, I gotta go. I'm starving, and I got tons of homework to do." That was probably going a bit too far. Even she knew that.

"Really?" Accident or not, I was not about to become Super-Student and she knew it. "The new PJ?"

"I'm working on it. I'm working on it." Well, I was. A little. Very little.

She just nodded. I think she at least wanted to hold out for some hope.

"I'll see ya tomorrow, Mom."

I stood at the foot of her bed, thinking how I should give her a hug or something. I couldn't remember if I had ever hugged her. I probably did when I was little, but it had to have been a long time ago.

"Well, I'll be here," she sighed as she pulled the bed table around in front of her like she was going to finish her supper.

I left.

Chapter Twenty-three

"You suckin' up to Coach, Barnes? You think that'll get you more playing time?"

Brian had appeared from nowhere and was breathing down the back of my neck. I didn't have time for this. The first bell had rung, and if I wasn't Super-Student, I was at least going to be On-Time Student. I didn't need any more hassles.

"Outta my way, Carson." I stepped back and slammed the locker shut. My butt pushed into the side of his legs as I turned to move around him, but he didn't budge. He pushed his right hand up against the locker and braced himself, blocking my exit. That did it. My decision had been made. I had Power.

"I know, Brian. I know," I whispered in the most sinister tone I could create, emphasizing the word *know* each time.

"You know what?" Arrogance still rang in his voice, but his eyes showed interest. I glared at him and answered through clenched teeth.

"I know what you've been up to, and there are other people who might want to know, too. You just watch your step around me. You got a problem."

"You're the one with the problem, Barnes. You're the one with the attitude. Just what d'ya think you know about me?" His tone was filled with animosity, but he had relaxed his position and dropped his hand from the locker. I stepped around him and took a direct line toward Mrs. Jordan's classroom, pausing at the door briefly to look back at him through the bodies passing between us.

"Mike Romano," I called across the hall to him before I stepped into the classroom.

All through English I sat in the back of the room, wondering what had possessed me to be so stupid, trying to decide what my next move was going to be. The problem was I didn't have one. Kyle kept grinning at me like we shared some secret, which I guess we did, sort of. I ignored him. I kept looking at Henry, thinking maybe there was some advice in that logical brain of his. He ignored me.

For the first time in the history of English class, probably any class, I dreaded the ending bell. When it rang, both Kyle and Henry left without a word to me, out the door before I had even moved from my seat. I hoped Mrs. Jordan would ask me to stay after class. She should have. I hadn't done my homework. Whatever it was. In fact, I still owed stuff she'd given me the day I ended up with her journal. Return her journal? Nope. I wasn't ready for that. I could've asked her for extra help, but she would've known something was up. Maybe I could've asked her something about the play we'd been reading. But I didn't read and hadn't been listening, so I had no idea what to ask a question about. Except maybe drugs. Shakespeare's plays always had drugs in them somewhere.

"Mrs. Jordan, can I ask you a question?"

I needed to stall for time. I wanted Brian in his next class before I left her room. At that moment, even Mrs. Jordan was less scary than dealing with him. In fact, after what I'd read in her journal about him . . . *What is wrong with that child? It's more than just being spoiled . . . arrogant, hot-tempered, unpredictable* . . . maybe even she wouldn't mess with him. *If corporal punishment were still allowed, I would have smacked Brian Carson right there in the hall today.* On the other hand, maybe she would. Not me. At least not right then. He was ticked. Right then I needed time.

"Of course you may, PJ." She seemed surprised. I guess she should have been. "Something about the homework?"

Great. What homework? I ignored the question.

"I was just wondering about Shakespeare and drugs. I mean his plays have a lot about drugs in them, don't you think? Last year, it was this sleeping potion, and now we have this stuff that makes people do crazy things. You think maybe Shakespeare did drugs?" I was trying to sound curious, but, frankly, I didn't care.

"Well, PJ, we don't really know a lot about his personal life. I suppose he might have." She spoke slowly. Her voice sounded cautious. "Why the interest?"

"Well, if he's so great and all, and he does drugs, why do we make such a big deal today about drugs?" I was struggling for conversation. It was beginning to sound like the smart-ass questions of a Kyle Hawkins or the "let's get the teacher off the track" approach of a Henry Rose.

"It's really very different, PJ. For one thing, Shakespeare's stories are not real, and the potions and drugs he refers to are products of his imagination, albeit perhaps based somewhat on actual substances. Also, if we explore the ramifications of the 'drugs' he uses, we can see that—"

Just then the bell rang signaling the start of the next class. Safe. For the moment. I glanced up at the clock.

"Could you give me a pass? I'm late."

She stared at me for what seemed like hours, probably at least five seconds, before she nodded her head slowly up and down. She peered over her glasses like she was staring through me, trying to figure out what had just taken place.

"Okay, PJ. Sure." She picked up the purple notepad of passes and scribbled my name and her initials on it and handed it to me without another word.

I fled the room.

But I was in no hurry. I had no fear of bumping into Brian at that point and no interest in being in math class. My locker, the lobby bulletin board, and the water fountain were convenient stops along the way, but my procrastination worked against me. As I turned the corner by the library, there was Mike Romano, standing in the hall outside Mr. Fowler's classroom.

"Good work, Barnes."

"I'm late for math," I muttered as I reached for the doorknob. He stepped in front of me and grabbed the pass out of my hand.

"No, no, no. You are official." He laughed as he waved the pass in front of my face. "C'mon, let's talk." He moved quickly toward the boys' bathroom at the end of the hall. I followed like a faithful servant.

"I heard you got a ride yesterday with Lockwood. Nice touch. I don't know how you managed it, but that was good. Damn good."

"He gave me a ride to the hospital. That's all."

"Damn nice of him, too, wasn't it?"

"What's the big deal? He gave me a ride."

Mike leaned against the sink, his arms folded across his chest.

"Marston saw you getting into Lockwood's car. And he saw that Carson saw you getting into Lockwood's car."

For chrissakes, were these guys everywhere? Didn't they have anything better to do than wander around spying on people?

"This is perfect, Barnes. Carson'll believe you. No doubt about that. Your credibility went sky-high." He lifted his left arm and tapped his index finger against his lips, like he was thinking. His arm dropped again, and he nodded as though he had answered his own question.

"You gotta do this today, Barnes," he continued. "The timing is right. Carson won't want anything to mess up his playing time at tomorrow's game. Today. You understand?"

I knew then that I was going through with it. Why not? I shrugged my shoulders.

"Sure."

"Go to class, Barnes," he said as he took the pass from his pocket and pressed it into my hand, folding my fingers over into a fist. "I wouldn't want to hold up your education."

My assurance to Mike meant nothing. I had no plan. I needed time.

At the end of fourth period, I was tempted to ask Mrs. Hempstead if I could stay in the art room. I hadn't seen Brian since our incident outside Mrs. Jordan's room, but, with luck, and some good timing, I could avoid him for the rest of the day.

I glanced toward the front of the room. The second bell was about to ring, and Mrs. Hempstead was nowhere to be seen. Maybe she didn't have a class fifth period. I hadn't ever noticed.

"C'mon, PJ. You better get going. You're already late for your next class."

Her voice came from the back of the room. I glanced over my shoulder. There she was, wiping off the edge of the sink on the back counter.

"I got lunch," I answered. I made no attempt to move.

"Well, so do I." She dropped a paint-stained rag on the counter and headed toward her desk. She opened a drawer and pulled out a pink plastic lunch bag. "Let's go so I can lock up here. I'm famished."

I wasn't hungry at all. I had other things to think about.

"C'mon, c'mon, c'mon, PJ Barnes," she said as she moved toward the door. She sounded like she was trying to joke with me. "Since when did you become Picasso?"

"Can't I just stay here and work?" I was trying to sound serious, but I heard the surliness in my own voice. She must have heard it, too.

"No, you may not," she snapped.

Maybe she really was hungry. She was holding the door open with her right shoulder and waving with her left hand, a sweeping movement which formed a large semicircle in the air.

"Okay, okay."

I picked up the project I was working on, a pencil drawing of a tree, one that grew sort of upside down, where the branches went into the ground and the roots spread upward toward the sky, and crumpled it into a thick ball. You know, it was a stupid thing to do. The picture was almost done, and it was pretty cool. I grabbed my backpack with my left hand and threw it over my shoulder as I tossed the ball into the wastebasket across the room.

"It wasn't very good anyway," I scoffed as I brushed past her. I heard the door close with a slam behind me. I didn't look back.

I stormed down the hall toward the cafeteria. The noise of clattering dishes greeted me as I turned the corner by the kitchen. So did Brian Carson.

"Not so fast, dork," he shouted as he grabbed my arm. "You got some explaining to do."

"No, Carson, *you* got explaining to do," I threw back in his face. "I'm not the one doin' business with lowlife." That was not quite true since Mike Romano had offered me money. I tipped my head toward the cafeteria full of students. "You really wanta talk here? You want me to *ex*-plain? Right now? Right here?"

He released his grip on my arm just enough for me to back

away, readying for my escape, but not before he caught my wrist and leaned into my face.

"Right after school," he snarled. "Before practice starts. You meet me in the parking lot at my Jeep." He squeezed my wrist tightly and then flung it aside. "You understand?"

"Don't you worry," I responded scornfully as I stepped to the side and slid between two students carrying their lunch trays. "I'll be there."

"I mean it," he hollered after me as I slipped into the cafeteria line. "You better be there."

"I'll be there," I muttered to myself. "I'm probably dead meat, but I'll be there."

Chapter Twenty-four

I was getting my jacket from my locker when I heard Mrs. Jordan call to me from down the hall. I was beginning to think I should ask for a locker change.

"PJ, may I see you for a moment?"

Great. Was I supposed to stay after school again? Probably. Since my mother's accident, I'd lost track of whether or not I was supposed to stay after school to work. Not that it ever mattered before. Mrs. Jordan hadn't said anything about me coming in, or not coming in, so I figured she had forgotten, too. Or maybe she thought I was spending all my time at the hospital. Which I really wasn't.

I trudged down the hall. She had already gone back into her room, but she was waiting for me just inside the door. It didn't look like she was expecting me to stay.

"Yeah?"

"Are you okay?"

"Yeah. I'm fine."

"You sure?"

"I'm fine. I'm fine." What did she want from me?

"Well, PJ, I'll get right to the point. I think you have my journal."

How was I getting out of this one? I had planned to give it back to her. But that was before I saw what she wrote about me. Now I couldn't. Spite? Anger? Embarrassment? I don't know. I just couldn't.

"I don't know what you're talking about."

"My blue journal, PJ. The one I've been missing for over a week. I think you have it."

"I didn't take it," I mumbled, looking down at my boots.

"I didn't say you took it." She sounded exasperated. "I said I think you have it. Maybe you don't even know you have it. Will you look, please?"

"Look where?"

I could hear her taking a deep breath, sucking air up her nose. She sounded annoyed. I wanted to look up at her, to see if she looked angry, but I didn't dare.

"Wherever you put your homework, maybe? Your locker? At home? Will you at least look?"

"Sure, yeah. I guess I can do that." There was a long pause. I could still hear her breathing. I wasn't.

"Can I go now?" I looked up slowly, waiting for her response.

She shrugged and nodded. I slipped out the door and headed for the nearest exit.

By the time I left the building, the last of the yellow buses was turning on to School Street. I walked through the faculty section of the parking lot, where a couple teachers were getting into their cars. At the outside edge of the parking area, Brian was leaning against his Jeep, his arms folded across his chest. The sun was just low enough so that I was looking directly into it and couldn't see his face. I walked across the asphalt, my heart thumping in my chest. I had no plan. As I got closer, he stepped away from the car and planted his feet solidly beneath him, his hands on his hips.

"So what is it, Barnes? Let's get this settled. We got practice." A slight grin, almost a sneer, grew across his face. "I told Coach I'd be a few minutes late. How about you?"

He had opened the door of opportunity. I walked in boldly.

"Oh, I think Coach'll understand." I tried to sound nonchalant. Not indifferent, just unconcerned.

"Understand what?"

"You, Carson. I think maybe he'll understand you just a little bit better. I think maybe he'll see you for what you really are." I paused. "A fake."

He grabbed my jacket and threw me against the side of his car. My knees buckled beneath me as I hit the metal. I had expected him to be pissed, but I figured the parking lot was safe. Out in the open. People around. I was wrong.

"Hey," I gasped.

His face was almost purple. He was an arrogant sonofabitch, but I'd never seem him this angry. He pulled me away from the car, his hands still clenched onto the front of my jacket.

"I—don't—like—threats, you asshole," he bellowed into my face.

"It's not a threat." I was gasping for air. "You pay Mike Romano what you owe him, or I tell Coach you're on drugs."

He released his hold on me and began pacing back and forth, one hand balled up into a fist that he kept tapping on the side of his head. Not hard. Just like he was trying to think, to shake some thought loose.

"I don't have anything to do with Romano."

I straightened up and picked up my backpack from where it had fallen off my shoulders when he grabbed me. My arms were shaking as I slid one strap over my right shoulder.

"Then Hawkins or Marston or whoever it is you deal with. But in the end it all comes down to Romano . . . and you know it. That's who wants the money."

He continued to pace, and a long silence filled the air between us. Suddenly he wheeled around and pounded his right fist onto the hood of his Jeep. Twice. Then, slowly, he turned back to face me.

"What's in it for you, PJ?" His voice was quiet and even. He had calmed down, almost too quickly. It was also the first time I remember him calling me PJ.

Suddenly I felt like dirt. Money? Was I really going to tell him I was doing this for money? Forty bucks already didn't seem like enough. Because he annoyed me? Ticked me off? Which he did. That I was afraid of Romano? Which I was. Right then I just wanted out of the whole damn mess. But there was no turning back.

"You're the one with the problem, Carson. You figure it out. I'm goin' to practice."

As I stormed across the parking lot toward the gym entrance, I kept expecting an arm to grab me around the throat. Instead, I heard a car door slam, and when I turned around, Brian's Jeep was speeding toward the exit.

Chapter Twenty-five

"You comin' to the game anyway?" Henry asked as we waited for English class to begin. Mrs. Jordan's room was open, but she wasn't there.

"Not sure," I told him. I hadn't gone to practice the day before after all. When I saw Kyle and Larry waiting near the locker-room entrance after I had left Brian, I ducked through the pool gallery and out the side door to the upper parking lot. I was tired of people. I just wanted to go home. Which is what I did. Even Frank and peanut butter were looking pretty good, except Frank wasn't around when I got home. I'd fixed a peanut-butter-and-jelly sandwich, watched some television, and then headed to the hospital. Frank was there.

"Lockwood'll expect you to be there," Henry continued. "Even if you can't play."

That's the rule. If you miss a practice just before the game, you don't get to play. But I didn't play much anyway, so what difference did it make?

"Carson ever show up?"

"Yeah, eventually," Henry answered slowly, eyeing me suspiciously. "How did you know he was late?"

I ignored the question. Apparently no one had seen us in the parking lot. Or at least no one who cared.

"Too late for practice to count?"

Henry shrugged his shoulders. I persisted.

"Think Coach'll play him anyway?"

Henry shrugged again.

"Why all the interest in Carson? I thought you couldn't stand him."

"I can't," I assured him.

The bell rang just as Mrs. Jordan came into the room. As she reached around to push the door closed, Kyle Hawkins slid in behind her.

"Hey there, Mrs. Jordan. Good morning." He wasn't really being flip. Just overly friendly. Mrs. Jordan looked bored.

"Good morning, Kyle. Glad to see you could join us this morning." She didn't sound sarcastic, but her point didn't go unnoticed. Kyle was absent more than he was in school.

As he slid into the desk next to me, he carefully placed a copy of *A Midsummer Night's Dream* on my desk. When I questioned him with my eyes, he motioned for me to open it. I lifted up the cover, and inside there were two twenty-dollar bills. I closed the book slowly, trying not to attract any attention, wondering if Henry had seen. I stared straight ahead. As Mrs. Jordan began handing out a vocabulary test, I slipped the book into my backpack and retrieved the copy I had been assigned just as Tracy Johnston dangled a copy of the test over her shoulder. I pulled it out of her hand and set to work.

Twenty minutes later, as Mrs. Jordan collected the tests, I was still pretending to be checking over my answers. I had finished the test quickly and spent the rest of the time trying to figure how I was going to explain the money to Henry if he asked. I was sure he would. I reluctantly passed the test forward.

"Okay, class, let's continue with the play. Any volunteers to read today?"

I raised my hand.

"PJ?"

She was surprised at my offer. I suspect the whole class was. I could feel Henry staring at me.

"What part would you like?" she continued.

"Whatever," I answered as I slouched down in my seat and opened up my book. "It doesn't matter." It didn't.

"Well, then, how about Oberon?"

"Cool, Barnes," Kyle blurted out, loud enough for everyone in the room to hear. "You get to be a fairy." A few kids laughed. I stared into the book, the one without forty dollars tucked inside.

"That's enough, Kyle. I don't hear you volunteering."

"Not a chance."

"Henry," Mrs. Jordan asked, moving on. It wasn't easy to throw her off track. "What about you?"

"Sure," Henry answered slowly. "I'll read." I could feel his eyes on me. PJ Barnes volunteered for nothing in class, this one or any other. My tactic for *diversion*, third word on the test, was failing miserably.

Ten minutes later, in the middle of Oberon starting to feel sorry for Titania, the phone rang. Ten seconds later I was on my way to the office.

I trudged slowly down the hall. I was in no hurry. Every time I went to the office, I ended up in detention. What had I done? Surely Brian hadn't turned me in for hassling him. No way.

"Mr. Cummings is waiting for you," Mrs. Fisher announced as soon as I walked into the office. She hardly looked up from her computer. "Go on in."

My heart thumped as I went through the little swinging door at the end of the counter that separates Mrs. Fisher from the students. You would think I'd be used to visits to the office by now. But you never get used to them. I hadn't been late. I hadn't mouthed off to any teachers, at least not much and not lately. I wished I'd stopped at my locker and stashed the money. Maybe it was my mother. Maybe the hospital had called. Maybe something had gone wrong, and she was worse, not better.

I sucked in my breath and turned right, heading down the short hall that leads to Mr. Cummings's office. As soon as I turned, I could see Coach Lockwood sitting in a chair. His back was to the opened door, and I could hear a man's voice, but it wasn't his. It didn't sound like Cummings's either. Before I even got to the door, Mr. Cummings came into view. He looked up from his desk and beckoned for me to come in.

"C'mon in, PJ," he said as he motioned toward an empty chair next to Coach. "Sit."

I walked through the doorway, and my stomach tightened as a gray uniform sitting in the chair to the right caught my eye. I sat down in the wooden chair next to Lockwood.

"Officer Taylor would like to ask you some questions, PJ."

"About what?"

I looked at Lockwood. What was he doing there? Had Brian gone to him, whining about me? He might have. I wouldn't put it past him. But I had forty dollars in my backpack. He had to have taken me seriously. He had to have paid up. He wouldn't do that and then confess. Would he?

Maybe it was a trap.

"You're not in trouble, PJ," Lockwood said. "Officer Taylor is hoping you can give him some information. That's all."

"Mr. Lockwood is here for you, PJ," Cummings offered. He must have noticed how I kept staring at Coach. "We couldn't locate your stepfather, and with your mom in the hospital, we thought maybe you would want someone here for you."

"I thought I wasn't in trouble." Obviously this wasn't about my mother.

"You're not," the uniform explained. "I just want to ask you some questions."

"I don't know anything." I tried not to shift in my chair.

"He hasn't asked you anything yet," Mr. Cummings pointed out.

"I don't know anything about anything."

"It's okay, PJ. You're not in any trouble." Lockwood paused, turning to the uniform for assurance. "He isn't, is he?"

"I don't think so," the officer answered. That was not particularly reassuring. "I want to ask you about your relationship with Mike Romano."

"I don't have a relationship with Mike Romano." Which was not exactly true, I guess. But it's not like we were friends or anything.

"Well, that's not what I hear," the officer continued.

Lockwood turned in his seat toward me. "You hangin' around with Mike Romano and his gang?"

I didn't think Larry and Kyle were enough to call a gang. I shrugged my shoulders and looked at the floor.

"Not really."

"And what does 'not really' mean?" he practically shouted, gripping the arms of his chair.

"Mr. Lockwood, maybe we better let Officer Taylor handle this."

Lockwood nodded and turned back in his seat and began tapping the fingers of his left hand lightly on the arm of the chair. It was annoying, and I wondered if the uniform thought so, too.

"We're looking for some help, PJ. We were hoping we could count on you to be that help."

"What kind of help?"

"Look, PJ. I'm taking a chance coming here and talking to you like this, taking a risk that you can be trusted. Can I trust you?"

"What kind of help?" I looked straight at him. Where were we headed here? "And why me?"

The officer slid forward toward the edge of his seat, like we were going to share some great secret. He rested his elbows on his

166

knees and folded his hands together in the open space between them.

"Can I trust you?" His voice was almost a whisper.

I wondered where this "Officer Goodguy" routine was going.

"I dunno. What're we talking about?"

He took a deep breath in through his nose and blew it out slowly, almost like he was exhaling a drag on a cigarette. I wondered if he smoked.

"Okay. Here's the deal. We've had a series of problems reported in the Bradford area. Some petty theft and some vandalism. We think Romano is at the center of these problems. We've also been watching him for some drug activity. Our problem is we have lots of theory and no proof."

"So why me?" I wasn't surprised to hear Mike was a suspicious character in the eyes of the law, but I needed to protect myself. Maybe the forty dollars in my backpack would be considered blackmail money.

"Well, PJ, we look at it this way. You've been seen hanging around with Romano, both in and out of school." At this point he looked at Mr. Cummings, who nodded in agreement. Only Lockwood seemed surprised at this observation.

"But only recently," he added. "Just within the last week."

This guy was good. He'd done his homework, and I was beginning to feel uncomfortable. My stomach was in knots. I tried not to stare at my boots.

"So," he continued, "we think you and Romano can't have a solid relationship yet. In fact, we aren't really sure what you are doing hanging around with him."

My stomach settled down somewhat.

"And, by all accounts, you never seem too at ease around him. In fact, we heard he ticked you off a little." He sat back in his seat and sort of laughed. I didn't see anything funny.

"I'm a little confused here," Lockwood stated loudly. "Just what is it you want PJ to do?" He was taking his surrogate parent role way too seriously at this point.

"We want you to work with us, PJ. Provide information for us. Help us to get proof." He spoke slowly, looking directly at me.

I couldn't believe what I had heard.

"You want me to be a snitch?" PJ Barnes was being asked to be an informer? I dug my hands into the arms of the chair to keep myself in the seat. "You're crazy."

"I hope not, PJ. We've been waiting for the right person to come along. We think that person is you."

"What makes you think you can trust me? What makes you think I won't run out of here and find Romano and tell him to watch out, tell him to lay low? What do you know about me anyway?"

Who did he think he was? Did he think I could be flattered into going along with him? He was just another person who wanted something from me. No one can be trusted. Certainly not the cops.

The laughter in Taylor was gone. His face was frozen into a mask, and his eyes pierced through me. When he spoke, his voice was calm, but firm.

"Two reasons," he began. "First of all, we know a lot about you, PJ. We know you're smart but a terrible student. We also know you're angry a lot and moody and that you're a loner. You have friends, but no best friend. Consequently, loyalty is not a big

168

issue for you." He paused as though he was deciding whether or not to add something. "However, we also know that at least one of your teachers thinks you're basically a decent person who can be trusted to do the right thing."

I was thrown into silence. As bad as it all sounded, when somebody came right out and said it like that, I had to admit it was all true. Except for that last part. I couldn't imagine any of my teachers thinking of me as someone to be trusted. I glanced sideways at Lockwood. Him? Not likely.

"Who?"

"Who what?"

"Who thinks I can be trusted?"

He slid back in his chair and looked at Cummings. Mr. Cummings bit his lower lip like he was thinking whether or not he should tell. I wondered if *he* felt like he was being asked to be a snitch.

"Mrs. Jordan," Mr. Cummings admitted slowly. "She was the only one I asked, PJ. Her opinion carries a lot of weight around here."

"Mrs. Jordan?" I whispered. This was sounding more and more like a trap. Mrs. Jordan thought I was a loser. I had written proof of that. I could pull her journal right out of my backpack and wave it around and shout, *You want to know what Mrs. Jordan really thinks of me? Just read this.*

"Yes, PJ, Mrs. Jordan," Cummings repeated.

"I don't believe it." I looked at Lockwood. He was no help. He looked as confused as I felt.

"Well, whether you believe it or not, it's true," Cummings emphasized again.

I stared at my boots once more. Time. Time. I needed time to think. What help could I be anyway? Petty theft and vandalism were pretty good guesses, but it had to be outside of school. I would have heard stuff if anything was going on in school. Drug stuff? Romano was a dealer. Everybody knew that. But wasn't that what those dogs were for? They'd been in sniffing around a couple times already this year. Of course everybody knew when they were coming. I guess Romano could have avoided that easily enough.

Nobody said a word for a long time, except Lockwood's fingers. He was tapping on the arm of the chair again.

"Mr. Lockwood," Cummings said quietly.

I glanced up to see Cummings tapping his fingers in the air. Coach quit instantly. I looked at the officer.

"So what's the second reason? You said you picked me for two reasons. If the first one is that I'm a loser who can be trusted, what's the second reason?"

I think he was just waiting for that question, like it was an ace up his sleeve. He didn't bat an eye and answered me quickly.

"Your mother."

"Huh?" I wasn't expecting that answer.

"It's a little premature to be certain, and we may never actually have any proof, but we think Romano caused your mother's accident."

"What?" My conversation with Romano about his car flashed back into my mind. I had bought his explanation. I think I still did. "What makes you think so?" Maybe Officer Goodguy just wanted me to think he did.

"Well, I said we didn't have any proof. Just some circumstantial evidence, and I admit that even if he did, we aren't too sure it was intentional. The worst charge against him would be leaving the scene of an accident. But even so, I can't help but think maybe you would not want to be doing business with someone whose irresponsible behavior put your mother in the hospital."

"What makes you think I'm doing business with Romano?"

"Are you?"

I shifted uncomfortably in my chair.

"Not exactly."

"What is that supposed to mean?" Lockwood was on the edge of his seat. "That kid is a loser."

"Mr. Lockwood!" Cummings interrupted him sharply. "Mike Romano is still a student in this school."

Lockwood glared at him.

"Nobody on my team should be hanging around with the likes of Mike Romano." His voice got loud and his face turned at least three shades of red. Coach was on a roll. "Anyone on my team caught with drugs or hanging around those who are known to use them is done, finished, without question." He clapped his hands, like he was putting an exclamation point at the end of his statement.

I was glad that the attention had shifted away from me, at least for a moment. I thought about telling him and Cummings and Officer Goodguy what I did know about Brian, especially Coach. Maybe he'd have a new understanding of the word *loser*. Maybe then they wouldn't be so interested in me and what I could or couldn't do for them. Maybe they could convince Brian Carson to be the snitch. But then, I had forty dollars in my backpack.

"That's enough, Barry," Mr. Cummings snapped. "Calm

down." He turned his attention back to me. "What does 'not exactly' mean, PJ?"

"I did him a favor, that's all. I didn't buy anything from him." The scowl on his face said he didn't believe me. "I didn't," I blurted out in self-defense. "I may be a loser in a lot of ways," I said sarcastically as I glanced at the officer, "but I'm not a druggie. I just gave somebody a message. It wasn't important."

I was digging a hole, and the dirt was sliding down into the hole around me.

"What kind of a message?" Cummings asked.

"Nothing important, I told you." I could hear the hostility in my voice. I was feeling trapped. My boots drew my attention once again.

"It's okay, PJ," Officer Goodguy said, coming to the rescue. "I believe you. If it wasn't important, then it wasn't." He paused. I could hear Lockwood tapping his fingers again. "Look. You think about what I asked. No pressure, I promise." He stuck a card out, holding it low so I could see it without raising my head. "You think you can help me out, you give me a call."

"Yeah, sure," I answered as I took the card and slid it into my jeans pocket. I glanced up at Cummings. "Can I go now?" He looked at Officer Goodguy, who nodded.

"Stop at the front desk and ask Mrs. Fisher for a pass."

As I left the office, I heard Coach call out after me, "See you at the game, PJ."

Chapter Twenty-six

"You in trouble?"

Billy was leaning on his crutches, peering over the carrel in the library where I was hiding ninth period, trying to decide whether or not I was going to the game.

"Huh," I grunted as I looked up.

"Is that a yes or a no?"

"Nah."

"Everybody's heard about your visit to the office this morning. With the police, and Lockwood there, too. And you've been avoiding me all day. I figure something's up."

"Nah, they were just asking me about my mom's accident."

"They know who ran her off the road?"

I dropped my head onto my arms and rolled it back and forth. Everybody had a theory. "We don't know that somebody ran her off the road," I muttered into my arms. "They don't know *what* happened. She doesn't remember." I raised my head. "And I haven't been avoiding you." I hadn't. I was avoiding a lot of people, but he wasn't one of them.

"Well, Henry seems to think you're avoiding us."

I had been avoiding Henry. I wondered how much he had seen in English this morning. Had he seen the money Kyle gave me?

"Well, I'm not."

"Aren't you supposed to be in Spanish?"

I was impressed with Billy's ability to change the subject without missing a beat.

"Substitute," I offered, as though that explained everything.

Just then the bell rang and bodies started shuffling though the carrels and stacks toward the library exit.

"C'mon, PJ, game time." He shifted his weight and adjusted his crutches under his arms.

I didn't move.

"You gotta go, PJ. You gotta be there," he added.

"Why?"

"Who's taking my place?"

I stood up and grabbed my backpack.

"Okay, Billy, sure. Coach'll put me right in for you. I bet he's real concerned about how to fill that ten or fifteen minutes you play."

It was mean. But Billy just grinned.

"Just think. You get my ten minutes plus your five. Not bad, huh?" He leaned forward and whispered. "Besides, a scout from Hartwick College is supposed to be at the game this afternoon. I don't think we ought to miss this for anything."

"Really?"

"For real."

"Carson?"

"That's the rumor. Of course the rest of the rumor is that Carson's father bribed the college to send somebody."

I swung my pack over my shoulder and headed toward the door.

"You're right. This *is* worth seeing."

Billy began the long hobble out to the soccer field, and I headed toward the gym. By the time I started changing, most of my teammates were already on their way out to the field. Only a couple guys were still in the locker room. Brian wasn't one of them. If a scout really was going to be there, he probably got himself excused from his afternoon classes so he could warm up or calm down or whatever explanation he thought his teachers would buy.

"So you made it." It was Henry. He was already in his uniform, leaning against the end of a row of lockers, his shin guards in his hands.

"Yeah, I made it," I answered as I stuffed my backpack into the locker and twirled the lock a couple times. Most guys didn't even bother putting their stuff into a locker, much less make sure the lock was in place. But I had forty dollars and Mrs. Jordan's journal, and until I figured out what I was going to do, they had to be under lock and key.

"That's good." His tone was a little too quiet, a little too serious. "I was beginning to wonder if maybe the police had come to take you off to jail."

"Ha. Ha," I laughed sarcastically. "Nice joke, Rose."

"Actually, I wasn't joking. What's going on, PJ?"

"What d'ya mean, 'what's goin' on?'"

"You're hanging out with Romano and his gang. Kyle's giving you money. The police show up and want to talk to you. Seems to me like something's going on."

"I'm not in trouble," I answered him quietly.

He didn't look convinced.

"I'm not. Really," I emphasized. "Life's just complicated."

"My dad says life's pretty simple. We just make it complicated."

Just what I needed. Advice from Henry's father. On second thought, I still wasn't sure if that forty dollars equaled a crime. Maybe I would be needing a lawyer soon.

"Well, Henry, I don't think your dad could untangle my life right now if I paid him a million bucks, which, by the way, I do not have."

"Well, you've got a few bucks. At least from what I saw in English."

Henry was opening a door for me, and maybe it was time not to be standing alone in the doorway. I heaved a big sigh and tapped my forehead three times against the cold metal of the locker.

"Kyle did—" I began. But before I could explain anything, Kevin Andrews appeared.

"C'mon, guys. Let's move it. Coach is pissed 'cause everybody's not out there ready to go. You guys seen Carson?"

Henry and I looked at each other. Brian Carson wasn't ready for the game? Henry let out a little laugh.

"Well, hey now," Henry said. "Guess the rumor of a scout

threw him over the edge. Somebody just might see what an idiot he really is."

As much as I agreed with Henry, something just wasn't right about this. What was it I had read in Mrs. Jordan's journal? *Something is wrong with Brian Carson . . . outbursts of rage . . . unctuous, ingratiating behavior one day . . . arrogant, caustic demeanor the next.* Maybe Mrs. Jordan was onto something. How could he not show up for this game? Yet I hadn't seen him since yesterday afternoon. Rage might have been a little too strong to describe our encounter, but he sure scared me. He had to have paid Romano what he owed him. Why else would Kyle give me the money?

"This isn't funny, Rose," Kevin snapped. "C'mon. We're short of players as it is. You guys better get out on the field before Coach has a heart attack. He's been yellin' for the last ten minutes." He wheeled around and disappeared out the door.

"Later?" Henry asked as he reached out and put his hand on my shoulder.

I nodded as I bent over and finished tying my cleats. When I stood up to leave, he was already gone.

Five to zero. Brian never showed, and Lockwood was so mad he was purple by the end of the game. But quiet. The yelling ceased halfway through the third quarter. He must have realized we were doomed. If he thought Brian's absence really had anything to do with the loss, he had a short memory. We always lost. The only thing different about the game without Brian was that the rest of us enjoyed it. The rumor of a scout turned out to be just that, a rumor. No one knew where Brian was, and nobody cared. Except maybe Coach. And me. Maybe Brian and Romano had had some blowup. As I left the field, Henry caught up with me.

"Some game," he shouted in my ear as he danced around me like he was involved in a boxing match.

"We lost, Henry, just in case you didn't notice."

"So what? Did you notice how much Coach played me?"

I didn't really want to point out that Coach didn't have much choice. With Billy injured and Brian missing, and Ryan Marlow apparently home sick, we all got to play most of the game. But he was right. The game was fun. I might have enjoyed it even more if I hadn't wondered all through the game where Brian was.

"Of course," Henry continued, "we were missing a few guys." He paused. "C'mon. I'm buying pizza. Billy's meeting me at Pete's."

"I gotta get my stuff," I mumbled as I headed toward the gym door. Only a few team members ever returned to the locker room. I was usually one of the many who went home in their uniforms.

"So is that a yes or a no?" Henry asked. When I shrugged in response, he took hold of my arm and gently pulled me to a stop.

"D'you know where Carson is, PJ?" he asked quietly.

"Why ask me?" I turned away and continued toward the locker room.

"The guys were talking at halftime. Somebody said they saw Carson and Hawkins in the halls today, and they didn't look too happy with each other. I just thought . . ."

I kept walking.

"You just thought what, Henry? That PJ Barnes and Kyle Hawkins are pals? That we're buds?"

"I saw the money, PJ. What's goin' on?"

"I don't know what you're talking about." I pushed through the metal door leading into the locker room.

Henry groaned as he followed me.

"C'mon, PJ. Cut the act. You think you're so tough. You're not tough. You're stupid." He sat down on the wooden bench between the row of lockers while I fumbled with the combination to my lock.

"I don't have a clue what's goin' on, but if you're mixed up with Romano, then you are stupid," he continued. "I saw money sticking out of the book in English class this morning. And I wasn't the only one. Talk about stupid. Like Kyle giving you a book wasn't going to catch people's attention?"

I pulled my backpack out of my locker and slammed the metal door shut so hard that the echo clanged throughout the room. He had nailed it, and I was so stupid I didn't even see it.

"That's it," I announced, more to myself than to Henry, as I rummaged through my pack.

"What's it?"

"That's it," I repeated. I couldn't believe my own stupidity. Henry was right. I was being stupid, but not for the reason he thought. Kyle wanted Henry, and anyone else, to see that money. "But why? Why?"

"Why what, PJ?"

"I don't know," I answered as I waved two twenty-dollar bills in front of Henry's nose. "But we're gonna find out."

"We?" Henry was on his feet.

"Yeah," I answered. "What were you saying about pizza?"

Chapter Twenty-seven

"No kidding?" Henry responded to my explanation of the forty dollars as we were just about to enter Pete's. "You are in a mess."

"You're a big help," I countered. "Tell me something I don't know."

"How about that you're an idiot?" He pushed the door open and waved me through with a grand, sweeping motion of his arm.

"Trust me. I know that," I snapped back.

It was warm inside, and the aroma of pizza dough and cheese and sausage made me realize how hungry I was. Pete's was very basic. A few booths lined the walls, and several odd-size tables with chairs that didn't match filled the center. It was never very clean, but never very dirty either. Jack—nobody knew who Pete was—ran the place and relied heavily on his customers to clean up after themselves. Some did. Some didn't. Thursdays were usually pretty busy after a game, but only a few customers were scattered among the tables and in the booths.

"Hi, PJ."

It was Amanda Cummings, sitting at a table with Tracy Johnston. Tracy didn't even glance up from her soda. They usually hung out with Henry's girlfriend, but he hadn't said anything about meeting Monica.

"How's your mom?"

"She's doin' okay."

"That's good. Billy looks like he's doing okay, too, huh?" She nodded toward the back, and I wondered if she was looking for an invitation to join us. Henry took charge.

"Well, girls, we have business. Hey, Tracy, if you see Monica later, tell her I'll call about nine."

So we weren't meeting Monica. I was glad. With Heather out of the picture, having Monica around was a pain. Of course I also realized at that point that I hadn't thought about Heather in at least seventy-two hours. I had hope.

"Hey, guys," Billy called from a booth near the back. "I ordered already. Hope that was okay." As we headed toward the booth, he gestured toward the counter. "But you gotta pay, Henry."

"That's why I'm here," Henry hollered back with a laugh as he headed toward the cash register.

That was the neat thing about the friendship between Henry and Billy. They were honest and direct with each other. I liked that.

I hung my backpack on a hook on the wall directly behind the booth and dropped into the seat opposite Billy, sliding in as far as I could to make room for Henry when he joined us. Billy was sitting sideways in the booth with his leg stretched out on the seat. He hadn't complained once about his injury, but he never looked very comfortable.

"Hey, you guys were great today. Even Henry," Billy said, smiling proudly. The fact that we lost didn't seem to matter to him either.

"Yeah, we were, weren't we?"

"I think it was 'cause Carson wasn't there," he continued. "You know how distracting Brian can be with all that yelling and everything. He makes it really hard for Henry to concentrate."

"Carson can be pretty hard for any of us to deal with," I added. On and off the field, I thought.

Billy leaned against the back of the booth, nodding in agreement.

"So anyone ever find out where he was?"

"Where who was? Carson?" Henry asked as he set three cans of soda on the table and slipped into the seat beside me.

"Yeah," I answered for Billy.

"You tell him?" Henry asked me as he popped up the tab on his Mountain Dew. Some of the drink squirted up on top of the can. He leaned over and slurped it up, making far more sucking noise than he needed to.

"Tell me what?" Billy asked as he reached for one of the cans of Pepsi. "You know where Carson was this afternoon, PJ?"

I popped the tab off my soda, pleased that Henry remembered I drank Pepsi, too.

"Nope," Henry answered for me. "But what he knows might have something to do with it. We just haven't figured that out yet."

182

"Will one of you tell me what you are talkin' about," Billy demanded as he pushed his soda to one side and tapped the index finger of his right hand on the table repeatedly.

Henry glanced over Billy's head, checking to see who else was in the place, and then dropped his head back down. When he spoke, his tone told Billy this was information that was not for the general public, and in less than a minute, and seemingly without taking a breath, he had told Billy a shortened version of everything it had taken me the whole walk from the school to convey. When he was done, Billy just sat there and stared at us.

"Well?" Henry demanded. "What do you think?"

Billy shifted his focus from Henry to me, to Henry, and back to me.

"Is this a joke?"

I shook my head back and forth.

"Are you crazy, Barnes? What d'ya think you're doing gettin' mixed up with Romano?"

"I didn't plan on getting 'mixed up' with him. It just happened."

"You took money from him. That doesn't 'just happen.' You gotta be a freakin' idiot."

His reaction was amazingly similar to Henry's. No wonder they were best friends.

"I didn't actually take money from him," I tried to explain. Henry's shortened version had left out a lot of details. "He gave it to me." I paused. "Well, actually, Kyle gave it to me."

Billy closed his eyes and shook his head like he was letting all the details shift around in his brain. When he opened them, they were focused on Henry.

"It's your fault. You should've kept him out of this."

"Me?" Henry blurted out. "What did I do?"

I was getting ticked. Billy was reacting like I was a little kid who needed protection, like I was taken in by the big, bad guys because I was too stupid or naive or something. He seemed more interested in my involvement with Romano than he was with Brian being on drugs. At least Henry had shown some concern for Brian when I told him that part of the story.

Billy shook his head and gave out such a big sigh, I could feel the air from across the table.

"No concern for Carson, huh?" I asked scornfully.

"I don't believe it," he stated simply.

"What do you mean you don't believe it?" Henry hissed quietly.

"Football players take steroids. Not soccer players," Billy offered calmly, as though that explained everything.

"And I thought *you* were the idiot," Henry remarked as he rolled his eyes at me.

"You got any proof?" Billy asked, ignoring Henry's observation. "Besides what Romano says?"

"The guy's a Neanderthal," Henry began. "And his behavior is classic. Mood swings. Rude rage . . ."

"'Roid rage," Billy interrupted.

"Huh?"

"It's called 'roid rage," Billy explained calmly. "Some of us listen in health class."

Henry tossed Billy's teasing aside.

"I think you're missing the point here," he responded.

"No, you are missing the point. Think about it. If Carson's

behavior says he's on drugs, then he's been on drugs since kinder-garten. He's a jerk, and he's always been a jerk."

"No," I interrupted emphatically, but quietly, almost in a whisper.

Henry and Billy both stopped talking and looked at me.

"What do you mean?" Henry asked. "Of course Carson's a jerk."

"Yeah, but it's different. He's different." Something is wrong with Brian Carson. "And I'm not the only one who sees it."

"What are you talking about? Who?" Billy asked.

"Mrs. Jordan," I whispered.

"Huh?" Henry's eyebrows squished together.

"Pizza for Rose," a voice hollered out from the counter.

"Make sense here, PJ," Billy demanded.

"Something she said, that's all. She knows he's a jerk, but she thinks he's acting weird, even for him."

"Mrs. Jordan told you she thinks Carson's a jerk?" Billy's tone told me he thought I was way out in left field on this one.

"Well, not directly."

"What do you mean 'not directly'?" Henry demanded.

"Look, it was just something she said. Never mind." I wished I hadn't brought it up. I felt a sudden urge to check the wall behind me to see if my backpack was still hanging safely on the hook. I wanted to make sure Mrs. Jordan's journal wasn't sticking out of the top yelling, "Here I am."

"Pizza for Rose."

I poked Henry with my elbow. "Are we gonna eat or what?"

Chapter Twenty-eight

By the time the pizza was almost gone, I had filled in the gaps in Henry's account of my situation. By the time Billy had heard the whole story, or at least as much as I had told Henry, he was a little more sympathetic, even though he still called me an idiot several times between bites. But he agreed that it looked like I had been set up, or at least used somehow. He was even willing to acknowledge that just maybe Brian was using steroids.

"So now what?" Henry asked me as he chewed on the last piece of crust.

"I'm not sure, but I've got to find Romano and find out if Carson paid up," I told him.

"What difference does it make?" Billy asked.

"It just doesn't make sense. If Carson paid up because he

thought I was going to tell Lockwood, then he would have shown up at the game, right?"

Henry shrugged his shoulders. "I guess so."

"If he didn't pay Romano," I continued, "then maybe he wouldn't have dared show up at the game because he would have thought I had told Coach."

"Yeah," Billy agreed. "So?"

"So me getting paid and Carson not showing up? They don't fit. I think Kyle gave me the money to make it look like I had told."

"You guys think Brian is really using steroids?"

Billy's question was directed not just to me, but to Henry, too. Henry and I looked at each other and nodded in unison as we turned back to Billy. Calling Brian by his first name didn't go unnoticed either. It was a sure sign Billy was showing some concern. And I was surprised to realize that I was glad. I wanted to be glad Brian hadn't shown up at the game. I wanted not to care whether or not he was on drugs. I wanted to hope Romano would beat the crap out of him. But I didn't. Instead, I wanted to know where he was, why he hadn't come to the game. Was I worried about him? Not much. I just didn't want any guilt.

"You gotta tell Coach, then," Billy stated.

"I don't think that's a good idea." They hadn't seen Lockwood in Cummings's office that morning. "He'd never believe me," I offered as an explanation. "Why would he? He's seen me and Brian together; he knows we don't get along," I added. "And now he thinks I hang out with Romano. He'd figure I was just trying to get Brian in trouble."

"Well, you just can't ignore all this," Billy commanded as he tapped his index finger on the table. I could almost hear Henry's father in his voice, insisting that one be responsible, meet his obligations. Billy had been hanging around Henry's house way too much, and Eldred Rose had not only potentially ruined his own son, but his son's best friend as well.

"I don't intend to," I snapped back. "But first things first. And Romano is first."

"Well, you don't have to wait too long," Henry announced quietly as he hunched down a little in the booth. "Look who's here."

Mike and Kyle were at the front counter. I leaned against the side of the booth so that Billy blocked my view of them, and theirs of me. But it was too late. Henry nudged me.

"They're heading this way," he whispered.

"Hey, there, Barnes. We've been looking for you," Mike said.

"Yeah?" I tried to sound unconcerned. "What for?"

"Where's Carson?"

I shrugged and looked at Billy, then Henry.

"Either of you guys seen Carson?" As though on cue, they both shrugged their shoulders and shook their heads.

"Nope."

"Not me."

I wanted to look directly into Romano's eyes, to sort of stare him down. But I couldn't do it. I looked at Kyle instead.

"Guess not," I added unnecessarily. "And we don't particularly care, do we, guys?" Their heads bobbed up and down in unison.

"Well, I care, Barnes. Let's go. We gotta talk." He tipped his head toward the exit. "Privately."

My bravado was melting quickly. I didn't want to be alone with these guys again. Three minutes in Romano's Mustang and I'd probably be selling pot to fourth graders by the next morning. Mrs. Jordan was right. *The only enemy PJ has stares back at him every day in the mirror.* All show. No substance.

"Whadda you guys want from me? I did what you wanted, didn't I? I've got forty dollars to prove it." I was trying to sound cool, under control, but my voice was shaking.

Romano wasn't flinching. In fact, he clenched his fists, pressed the sides of them onto the table, and leaned forward slightly.

"It didn't quite work out the way it was supposed to, Barnes. We're looking for damage control here." He paused, and in spite of a slight smile which formed as the edges of his mouth turned upward, his face clouded over. "The money is yours, P-J." He emphasized the *P* and the *J*, once again making fun of my name . . . and me. "You did what we asked. You played; we paid. But we paid in full, and Carson didn't. So . . . now we need you to—"

"Leave him alone."

Billy's voice startled me. For a few seconds I had forgotten he and Henry were there in the booth with me.

"This isn't your business, creep," Romano responded, not looking at Billy but keeping his eyes fixed on me instead.

I tried to look at Mike directly, but I just couldn't do it. I'd stare at him for two seconds and then find myself looking past him or glancing down at the pizza pan, where a lone piece of sausage stared back at me. I was grateful for Billy's support, and even more grateful that Henry, class clown and master of smart-aleck responses, had been silent. But these two were no match for Romano and Hawkins. And neither was I.

"I said leave him alone," Billy insisted.

This time Romano laughed.

"So what are you gonna do? Hit me with a fuckin' crutch?"

Henry was out of the booth in a flash.

"You unconscionable bastard," he yelled as his arms circled Romano's waist, pulling him backward, away from the booth. Only Henry would use a word from an English vocabulary list as he was about to start a fight that would surely end in his own death. And he thought I was the idiot?

Before I could slide out of the booth, Kyle blocked my way. He didn't seem too worried about Romano's ability to handle the situation. He didn't need to be. Henry was being flung from one side of Romano to the other, like a shirt flapping in the wind on someone's clothesline.

"You aren't goin' anywhere," Kyle sneered as he pushed me back into the corner of the booth, his left hand pressed against my throat. I didn't know if I was being strangled. It was a new experience. I just knew I couldn't breathe. Through blurred vision, I saw Billy struggling to his feet, but just as he reached for his crutches, Kyle did a side kick with his right leg and they went clattering onto the floor.

"All right, you guys. That's enough." Jack's voice boomed as he bolted through the swinging door from the kitchen, rolling pin in hand. "This ends, or I call the cops."

Kyle instantly released his hold on my throat but continued to block my exit. It didn't matter. I wasn't going anywhere. I leaned forward against the edge of the table and gulped in air.

"Call the cops. Call the cops," Henry's voice called out from somewhere behind Romano.

"Let 'im go," Jack barked as he waved the rolling pin at the end of his flour-covered arm. It was a little unclear who was supposed to let go. Henry's arms were still wrapped tightly around Romano's waist, but Romano had him pressed firmly against the wall, and Henry could hardly be seen.

"I said, let 'im go," Jack bellowed again, and then slammed the rolling pin down on the nearest table. The crack of wood on metal was deafening. Even Kyle jumped away from the booth at the noise.

Romano clamped his right hand onto Henry's left wrist and with a quick step to the side pulled Henry around in front of him and then slammed him back against the wall, where he instantly slid to the floor.

"You asshole," he said scornfully as he stepped over Henry's legs and headed toward the exit. Kyle waited until Mike was past Jack and then hurried to catch up with him.

"And I don't want to see you guys in here again," Jack bellowed after them. "Ever."

"You jerk," I said to Henry as I held out my hand to pull him to his feet. Billy was hobbling toward the back wall to pick up his crutches. "You okay?"

"Pretty stupid, huh?" It was more of a statement than a question. He was breathing hard, but there was no blood, no bruises, no life-threatening injury.

"He okay?" Jack's question was directed toward me, which didn't make much sense, since he could see for himself that Henry was alive.

"Yeah, he's fine."

"Good. Now you guys get out of here."

"What?" Billy blurted out as he arranged his crutches under his arms. "We didn't do anything." Which was not exactly true. In less than two minutes we had mastered the art of pissing off the local criminal element.

Jack pointed the rolling pin toward the door. "You've finished your pizza. Go on. Get out of here."

Chapter Twenty-nine

When Billy's mom offered to drop me off at the hospital, I was glad. It wasn't much of a walk from Pete's, but I had visions of a blue Mustang coming to a screeching halt beside me as Kyle's long arm yanked me into the backseat.

"Thanks, Mrs. Jackson," I mumbled as I opened the back door of the car and stepped onto the pavement outside the hospital's main entrance.

"You're welcome. Tell your mom I'll see her in the morning." Mrs. Jackson's voice was stiff with politeness. Billy had called her on Henry's cell phone after we'd left Pete's, and I don't know what he told her, but for the first couple minutes in the car, I thought maybe I should have risked meeting up with Mike and Kyle.

"I will. See ya later, guys."

"Sure you don't want me to hang out here with you, PJ?"

Henry asked. It was hard to tell whether he was trying to be the faithful friend or if he, too, sensed that Mrs. Jackson was pretty pissed. I didn't blame him. She treated me like her son's friend. She treated Henry like he *was* her son. On the other hand, I guess that wasn't so bad.

"Nah. I'll probably be here awhile. I'll see you guys in the morning."

I closed the door and headed toward the entrance as Mrs. Jackson pulled away. It was almost seven o'clock. My mom would probably be done eating supper. Maybe Frank was there. Our paths hadn't crossed too much the last couple of days. Mom hadn't even asked if we were getting along. I guess that was a good sign that she wasn't worried about dying anymore.

"Hi there, PJ. How ya doin' tonight?" It was Margie, sitting behind that glassless window. I shifted my backpack from my right shoulder to my left as I nodded slightly to her.

"Frank just left," she added as I moved through the open doorway and into the hall. My mom's room was on a side corridor to the left past the lounge and cafeteria. I had just passed the entrance to the lounge when I heard my name being called.

"PJ?"

As I turned, my backpack slid down my left arm. I grabbed the strap with my right hand and let the bulk of the pack drop gently onto the floor beside me, my fingers firmly wrapped around the back strap. A man wearing a Carson Construction Company T-shirt stood half in the lounge and half in the hall.

"You are PJ, aren't you?"

"Mr. Carson?" My question was ridiculous. I knew it was Brian

Carson's father. Anyone who ever went to a soccer game knew who Brian's father was. I think I was just surprised that he knew me, a minor player, a worthless teammate, a recent pain in the butt for his son.

"Boy, am I glad to see you," he continued. "Did Coach get my message?"

"Message?"

"I left a message with Mrs. Fisher. She said she'd try to get it to Coach Lockwood before the game." He was speaking fast, like he was out of breath. "He didn't get it, did he?" he asked before I had a chance to answer. He clenched his right hand into a fist and rapped it against the door frame. "Damn."

"I don't think so," I answered slowly. Nothing in Lockwood's behavior at the game indicated he had gotten any message. He spent the whole game pacing back and forth, shifting from anger to worry, hanging on to anger most of the time.

Mr. Carson looked at the floor and shook his head.

"We all wondered where Brian was," I offered quietly. It was true. Everyone had wondered where he was, but it was more curiosity than concern. And then it hit me. We were in the hospital. Mr. Carson was here in the hospital, in a waiting room. That meant that Brian was here.

Oh God, I thought. My stomach sank to my knees. What had I done? Had Romano beaten him up? I should have told somebody, anybody. But it didn't make sense. Even Romano didn't know where he was.

"Is Brian here? What happened?"

Mr. Carson turned back into the lounge. I followed. Nobody

else was there. He took off his hat and threw it on the floor as he sat down in a chair, the same one I had occupied for hours on Saturday. He braced his elbows on his knees and buried his face in his hands. Except for the balding head staring back at me, the scene reminded me of Frank worrying about my mom. I tossed my backpack onto the couch and sat down opposite him.

"Mr. Carson?" He didn't respond. "You okay?" No answer. "Is Brian okay?"

Slowly he lifted his head and nodded.

"Yeah, he's okay. Sort of. It's his hand," he explained slowly. "He's still getting some X-rays done. We've been here for hours. Everything takes such a long time." He looked up at me and shook his head. "I don't understand. I just don't understand. I came home early from work so I could go to the game, and there he was, out in the garage. He was so angry. And he wouldn't talk to me. I kept asking him what was wrong, but he kept yelling, and I couldn't understand what he was yelling about." He paused, staring at me with a puzzled look on his face. "You're his friend," he continued. "What happened?"

I was Brian's teammate. I was not his friend. Why Mr. Carson would even think that was beyond me. I had no answer for him. He didn't seem to notice that I hadn't answered.

"Everything was going so great," he continued. "Today's game was important. We even heard a scout was going to be there."

"There wasn't."

"Huh?"

"There wasn't any scout," I explained. "I don't know why anybody thought there was going to be."

"Well, Brian thought there was. He told me yesterday. And he was so excited. We thought it was his big chance. I don't understand it, PJ. He wouldn't have missed that game for anything."

I would have expected Mr. Carson to be angry that no scout had shown up. But he wasn't. He just sounded sad and confused.

I didn't want to talk about scouts and soccer games. I needed to know what was going on.

"What did he do to his hand?" I asked.

"Huh?"

"His hand," I emphasized, shaking my right hand a little in the air. "What's the matter with his hand?"

"Broken. I'm not sure how. I think maybe he bashed it into the side of his Jeep. But I'm not even sure about that." He stopped and looked at me again, like he was sizing me up, figuring out how much he should tell me. When he started to speak again, his voice was very quiet, like we were sharing a secret.

"He just kept yelling, and it didn't make any sense. He repeated over and over that it wasn't his fault, that he took care of it, that Lockwood wouldn't care, that he didn't mean it, that it was an accident, that they couldn't do this to him. PJ, I have no idea what he was talking about."

I shifted uncomfortably in my seat. I didn't know what he was talking about either, but I had a pretty good idea some of it related to me.

"I don't know, Mr. Carson. I don't really know Brian very well." Which was not exactly true. I knew he was a jerk and a bully who worked at making my life miserable.

"But you must. You're his teammate, aren't you?"

I wanted to tell him that my life did not start and end with the soccer team, but I don't think he would have understood. I shrugged my shoulders and stared at my boots. He didn't wait for a response.

"I know Brian has a temper. Maybe he gets it from me." He paused and shook his head again. "But he's never been violent. I don't think he's ever really gotten in a fight or anything like that."

He was right. A lot of kids were afraid of Brian, but I had never seen him in a fight. At least not a real fight. At least not until our incident in the parking lot. Mostly he was loud and obnoxious and pretty good at intimidating kids. I used to think his father was loud and obnoxious, too. But there, in the hospital, Mr. Carson seemed small and sad.

I was not about to discuss Brian's trouble, whatever that was, with his father. Luckily, a nurse appeared.

"Mr. Carson? Your son is almost ready to go home. Dr. Whitson would like to speak with you first, though, so if you would come with me, please?" She turned and swept away, expecting Mr. Carson to fall in step behind her.

"I'll call Coach later to explain," he hollered over his shoulder as he hurried after the nurse. "And I'll let Brian know you were here."

"Oh, that ought to be interesting," I muttered to myself as I turned down the hall toward my mom's room. "That'll just about put him over the edge," I added to no one in particular.

The door to my mom's room was slightly open, and I could hear voices as I approached the doorway. She was sitting up in bed, sipping from a cup, her dinner tray still on the bedside table pulled in front of her. She smiled as she saw me.

"Hi, sweetie. I've been wondering where you were. Look who's here."

"Hi, PJ."

My heart jumped. It was Mrs. Jordan. She was leaning against the windowsill with her arms crossed in front of her.

"Wasn't it nice of Mrs. Jordan to come visit me?"

"Yeah, sure." I tried to sound friendly. I don't think it worked. I never expected she would really come. I moved quickly to the left side of my mom's bed, staying as far away from Mrs. Jordan as I could get. I dropped my backpack onto the floor, out of sight, and leaned back against the empty second bed.

"We were talking about when I was in high school. Did I ever tell you she was my teacher, too?"

My face felt hot, and I wondered if these two chummy women noticed my embarrassment. I should never have read a word of Mrs. Jordan's journal. I should've burned it. I wanted to scream, "Were you talking about me, too? About my loser of a father who *tried so hard to ignore his responsibilities when poor Stephanie found herself pregnant?*" I wondered if my mom would have been so happy if she knew Mrs. Jordan thought she was *somewhat of a lost soul?*

"PJ? Were you listening to me?"

"Huh?"

"Did I ever tell you Mrs. Jordan was my teacher?" she repeated.

"Uh, maybe." Trapped. "Yeah, I guess so."

"Well, it's very nice of her to visit me, isn't it? You must have told her about my accident, huh?"

I shrugged. I wasn't in the habit of sharing my life with my teachers. She just knew.

"Oh, everybody knew about the accident shortly after it happened, Stephanie. I got a call from Mr. Cummings early Saturday evening. Everyone from school was quite concerned about you and"—she paused for a moment, and when I glanced up, she was looking directly at me—"about how PJ was doing."

That was news to me. But it also explained why Mrs. Jordan hadn't bugged me all week about my homework. She felt sorry for me. My face grew hot. My mother's accident had provided a convenient excuse, and it was damn embarrassing. Sure, I had done some homework while waiting to see if she was going to be okay. But she was going to be fine, and my newfound conscientious-student mode had quickly vanished. It was Thursday already, and I was back to doing as little as possible.

"PJ is doing just fine, aren't you, sweetie?"

"I'm okay," I mumbled. Why did she have to call me sweetie in front of Mrs. Jordan?

"Did he tell you he has a job?" When she saw Mrs. Jordan shake her head no, she added, "But he promised me it won't interfere with school. Right, PJ?"

I was sure I had told her that I didn't get the job, at least not yet. At the moment, it didn't seem important to remind her.

"You feeling better today, Mom?" I needed to change the subject, and I really was concerned about how she was doing. I wanted her home, although it was for selfish reasons. I was tired of coming to the hospital every night.

"I had a good day. My doctor says I'm doing as well as could be expected. I guess that's pretty good." She gave a little laugh. If she was making a joke, I didn't get it.

"Any thought on how long you will need to stay here in the hospital?" Mrs. Jordan asked.

Did she really care? She was probably just trying to be nice. I was already bored with the conversation.

"Hopefully, I'll be home by the end of next week. A lot longer before I'm back to work, though," my mom explained. No laugh this time. She smiled weakly at Mrs. Jordan and then turned her attention back to me. "So how was the football game?"

"Fine," I answered her. It was pointless to remind her that I played soccer, but the confused expression on Mrs. Jordan's face made me wonder if I should have. "Same old stuff. We lost."

"I thought you played quite well, PJ."

You could have knocked me over with a puff of smoke.

"Well, that's good to hear," my mom announced loudly. "The last I heard he was thinking about quitting."

"You were there?" My voice sounded hollow, like I wasn't really in the same room.

"Oh, only for maybe fifteen minutes," Mrs. Jordan explained. "Did Brian ever show up?" she added as an afterthought.

She was full of surprises.

"No-o-o," I answered slowly. Obviously she didn't know he was here in the hospital. Maybe I should have said something.

"That was pretty unusual for Brian, wouldn't you say?"

I looked down at my boots. I was surprised to find the laces were tied and only vaguely remembered tying them in the locker room.

"PJ?" It was my mom. "Mrs. Jordan was talking to you."

No question about it. My mom was feeling better. I was getting lectured. And in front of a teacher.

"Yeah, I heard her." I tried not to sound ticked. What was I supposed to tell her? Yeah, Brian Carson wouldn't miss a game . . . unless, of course, he had freaked out over being blackmailed and ended up in the hospital. And by the way, I'm pretty sure he's on drugs. You know. You've noticed something, too. Oh, sure.

"It's okay, Stephanie. I really need to get going anyway." She picked up her coat from where it had been draped over the back of the only chair in the room and slipped it on. "I do hope you will be able to go home soon," she said as she patted my mom's hand lightly. "I'll see you in class tomorrow," she added, nodding to me as she turned toward the door. I was relieved she was leaving.

As she reached the opened doorway, loud yelling erupted in the hall. It sounded like Brian, and maybe his father, but there were other voices I didn't recognize, and it was impossible to tell what anyone was saying.

"What's that?" my mom cried out.

Mrs. Jordan bolted out the door. Teacher instinct, I guess. I flew out behind her and immediately screeched to a halt to avoid crashing into her. I stepped to the right just in time to see two men holding Brian. Brian's face was almost purple, and his body heaved back and forth trying to shake loose from their hold.

"Get your fuckin' hands off me," he screamed.

A crowd of people began gathering in the hall as the struggle continued. One man in a shirt and tie had Brian's left arm pulled back behind him, while the other, a younger man in the kind of shirts the hospital people wear, braced himself in front of

Brian with one arm clenching Brian's right forearm and the other pressed against his chest.

"Please. Please. Don't hurt him," Mr. Carson begged. "Brian, stop it! Stop it!"

Brian didn't seem to notice his father was even there. His eyes were wide open, but they darted around the hall, focusing on no one, even when he was yelling. His face was twisted into an angry mass, and he was sweating more than I have ever seen anyone sweat even on the hottest day in summer.

"PJ? PJ, what's going on out there?" my mom called from behind me. She sounded frightened. Before I could move, Mrs. Jordan had stepped into the doorway, and from behind me, I heard her voice, calm and controlled.

"Someone got upset, Stephanie. That's all. It's over now."

Just then a nurse swept into my mother's room and closed the door. I was glad. I have to admit that, at that moment, I was more interested in the scene in the hall than in my mother. I think Mrs. Jordan was, too.

"She'll be okay." She nodded to me as we both turned our attention back to the end of the hall. Brian had quit thrashing and was breathing hard, his head dropped down so his chin rested on his chest. Even from twenty-five feet away we could hear the long gulps of air being pulled into his lungs. Together we moved closer, Mrs. Jordan drawn perhaps from concern for a student. Me? It was pure curiosity. It was also a mistake.

As Brian lifted his head and opened his mouth to draw in some air, his eyes landed directly on me, and they opened so wide that his eyelids disappeared. His shoulders began to heave and roll like a great ocean wave.

"You!" he roared, hurling himself toward me. The two men lunged forward with him.

"You!" he hollered again. "You fuckin' bastard!"

My heart stopped. Curiosity turned to fear. Brian Carson, the jerk, the bully, was mostly talk and not much action. His anger in the parking lot was nothing compared to this. This Brian was scary, and I *was* scared.

"You bastard! You bastard!" he kept shouting as the two men struggled to hold him back.

And then it happened. Mrs. Jordan stepped in front of me. It was the nicest thing anyone had ever done for me in my entire life.

"Go back into your mother's room, PJ," she said without looking at me.

I didn't move. My legs had turned to jelly, and my feet had turned to stone. When people talk about their heart in their throat, they're wrong. My heart was pounding like crazy, and it was sinking lower and lower toward the floor. I reached out to the side and felt the roughness of a plaster wall under the palm of my right hand. It was the only thing that felt normal at that moment.

"Go, PJ. Now," Mrs. Jordan commanded.

I didn't. I couldn't. My hand was glued to the wall. It was the only thing holding me up.

A flurry of arms and legs blurred before me and suddenly Brian was on the floor, facedown, his arms pinned behind him. His back heaved up and down, but his legs had quit kicking. He was moaning, almost crying. I had never seen anything like it in my life.

"Let's calm him down," the man in the shirt and tie called to a nurse, who turned and headed down the hall.

"What's wrong with him?" Mr. Carson asked, leaning forward slightly as he braced himself against the wall, panting hard, one hand against his chest. "What's wrong?" he repeated. He looked around like he expected someone to answer him.

"He's been taking drugs," I blurted out. A knot twisted in my stomach. The words had come out before I realized what I was saying.

Mr. Carson looked sharply at me. His lips turned downward into a scowl, almost a sneer. He looked amazingly like an older version of Brian.

"That's absurd. Why would you say that?" He stepped toward the men holding his son. "Brian would never take drugs."

"Right now, sir, his behavior says otherwise," said the younger man.

The shirt and tie looked directly at me. "You know what he's been taking?"

I stared at the floor. I had some ideas, but I really didn't know.

"Maybe steroids," I answered, almost in a whisper.

"My son does not take drugs, I tell you." Mr. Carson's voice was angry. He turned back to me. "Why would you say that? I thought you were his friend."

"Friend or no friend," the shirt and tie explained, "he's probably right. It sure explains this outburst."

Just then a nurse knelt down beside Brian and injected something into his arm. Seconds later a gurney appeared. Brian is not a small person, and I was wondering how they intended to lift him up when the gurney dropped to the floor beside him. His body had gone limp, and his eyes were closed, but I could still hear him moaning quietly.

"Easy," the younger man said to the man who had come with the gurney as they rolled Brian over and lifted him smoothly onto the rolling bed. In seconds they had disappeared down the hall.

The shirt and tie turned his attention back to me.

"What makes you think he's taking steroids?"

What was I supposed to say? Oh, I'm just part of a blackmail ring, the collection agency, the stooge for the drug dealers in town. Sure. I'll just spill my guts right here in the hospital hall, outside my mother's room.

"Well? You made a pretty serious accusation, son," the shirt and tie demanded.

Mr. Carson stepped toward me. He held his arms out in front of him, his palms turned upward like he was holding a book or waiting for me to give him something.

"You're not telling the truth, are you, PJ?" The anger in his voice had been replaced by a whining tone. Now he sounded as much like Brian as he looked like him. "You can't be telling the truth."

I just stood there.

"You can't be," he snapped, his anger returning. "Unless you're the one selling them. Is that it?"

His accusation was stupid. Still, I felt trapped.

"She knows," I said, pointing to Mrs. Jordan, whose arms were crossed in front of her, like she was cold. "You do, don't you?"

She didn't answer, but I swore she nodded her head up and down slightly as she glanced back at me with a puzzled look on her face. My heart was pounding, and I felt out of breath even though I hadn't moved an inch. Words flew out of my mouth before I could stop them.

"You thought he was acting weird this year, didn't you? You thought somebody ought to find out what was wrong." I could see her black-ink handwriting at the bottom of a page. Something is wrong with Brian Carson. Student Assistance Team referral?

"That so?" the shirt and tie asked, turning his attention to Mrs. Jordan. "You think this kid's right? If illegal drugs are an issue here, I have to notify the police."

"No, he's not right," Mr. Carson persisted.

"Well, we'll find out soon enough anyway," the shirt and tie answered.

"Well, I have no proof, but, yes, I believe there may be some truth to what PJ says," she confirmed. "Brian's behavior this year has been very erratic."

Mr. Carson glared at me as a nurse took him by the arm.

"Why don't you come with me," she urged him quietly, but in a way that said she meant business. "We'll see how your son is doing."

As he shuffled down the hall beside the nurse, he looked over his shoulder at me briefly, shaking his head as though I had just committed some horrible crime. I felt like I had.

"I'll have to inform the police. They may be contacting you both," said the shirt and tie.

"Of course," Mrs. Jordan answered, nodding.

He nodded to us both and then followed the nurse and Mr. Carson down the hall.

"Whew." Mrs. Jordan exhaled loudly. "That was just a little

more excitement than we needed." She paused slightly, and I swear that, at that very moment, she was smirking. "And you know, PJ, for a moment there, I thought you were dead meat."

I was rather impressed at her choice of words. However, considering I had practically peed my pants when Brian lunged at me, I found her sense of humor just a little warped.

Chapter Thirty

"You can put your pack on the backseat," Mrs. Jordan said as I heard the click of her Impala unlocking.

I didn't want her offer of a ride, but my mom insisted. She had freaked out when she heard what had happened in the hall. I told her I'd be fine, that Brian was probably in a straitjacket by then, or at least doped up enough to be harmless. Then Mrs. Jordan volunteered to take me home, and my mom was so pleased, I didn't know what else to do. On the other hand, there was Brian's father, still somewhere in the hospital, who probably figured I had single-handedly ruined his son's life. And who knew where Romano was?

So there I was, climbing into a rather nice, but very uncool car with my English teacher. At least it was dark by then, and nobody was likely to see me. I slid into the front seat and placed my pack between my feet.

"Well," she sighed as she slipped the key into the ignition and started the engine. Her car started so smoothly I almost couldn't tell it was running. I wondered when, or maybe I should have wondered if, my mom's car would be replaced. We'd never had a car that started quietly, or easily.

"Well," she said again. "That was something, wasn't it?" She leaned her head back against the seat, her hands folded in her lap. She didn't seem to be in a hurry to leave.

"Yeah," I mumbled. I wished I was walking home.

"You did the right thing, you know. It's not easy to tell a parent about the failings of his child. It was very courageous on your part."

I didn't feel very courageous. In fact, I was feeling pretty rotten. Would she call me courageous if she knew about the forty dollars? I waited for her to ask about her journal. She had to know I had it. Instead, she took a deep breath, put her car in gear, and drove out of the parking lot.

"You turn left," I offered as she approached the exit.

"I know where you live, PJ," she responded matter-of-factly.

"You do?"

"Bradford isn't that big," she answered.

I still thought it was odd. She couldn't possibly know where all her students live.

"I gave Mrs. Hadley a ride home from a meeting at church once," she explained. It was weird, like she knew what I was thinking. Mrs. Hadley was my neighbor. Did they drive down the street with Mrs. Hadley pointing out all the houses and explaining who lived where? I wonder what she said about my family. I remember having cookies at the Hadleys' house when I was little, but I hadn't even been in their yard in years.

"Oh." I couldn't think of anything to say. We rode toward the main intersection in silence. Conversation when you're alone in a car with your English teacher is not an easy thing.

"Well," she began after what seemed like a century of quiet. "I guess we're both probably glad tomorrow's Friday. I'm not going to get my homework done tonight either." It wasn't a complaint. Just a statement. But I thought it pretty interesting that she included me in her comment.

"My mom really liked you coming to visit." It seemed like a safe piece of conversation. It also got us away from talking about homework.

"I hope so," Mrs. Jordan said. "I always liked your mom."

"You did?" I wanted to kick myself. She sounded sincere, not like she was just trying to be nice. Maybe she didn't think my mother was a lost soul anymore. Then again, maybe she didn't know Frank.

"Yes, PJ. I did . . . and I do."

"Do you remember my dad . . . my real dad?" Stupid. Stupid. Stupid. Why did I ask that?

"Peter Barnes? Oh, yes, I remember him." There was almost a little laugh in her voice.

"A loser, huh?"

"No, PJ, not a loser. Just a little lost." Her tone had become serious.

"Like me?"

"No, PJ, not like you. Your father had a hard time making decisions, and maybe he didn't ultimately do the right thing. I don't know. It's sometimes hard to know what the right thing is."

I said nothing.

211

"But you're a different person," she continued. "You may not be making good choices right now, but I think you know that. And I think eventually you will do the right thing."

I had no response. If we were at school, I'd think I was getting lectured. I'd retreat into anger, or at least my surly state. But here in the dark, Mrs. Jordan didn't sound like she was lecturing me. I didn't even feel annoyed. I just felt sad. I wanted my mother at home, telling me I was grounded. I even wanted to see Frank with his nose in *Motor Trend*. I wanted to erase the picture in my head of Brian Carson, lunging toward me, his face purple with rage.

Neither one of us said anything as she braked slowly for the red light ahead. The turn signal inside the car blinked on and off, pointing to the right. I stared out the side window, feeling my eyes fill with tears. This was stupid. I hadn't really cried in years . . . over anything.

"That's odd," she said, more to herself than to me as we turned the corner. "That looked like a flash of light. Did you see it?" She had pulled over to the curb in front of the Midtown Market.

I had seen it. A flash of light toward the back of the store. What I also had seen was Romano's Mustang parked in the alley just before we turned the corner.

"What?" I just wanted her to drive away.

"A light from the back of the store. Maybe something's wrong. Did you see it?"

"No, I didn't see anything," I lied. I turned my head toward the front windshield, willing her to pull away from the curb. What did she think we should do? Hop out of the car and investigate? *Drive away*, I begged her in my head.

"I guess it's nothing," she said as she pulled away.

Whew. I didn't need to check out what was happening. I knew. I knew then why Larry took the job and why Mike said I'd have it before long.

I rode the rest of the way in silence. Mrs. Jordan was talking all the way, but I heard nothing. As she swung into the driveway, I spied Frank standing on the porch smoking a cigarette. He lifted his hand in a slight wave. I didn't know if it was for me or Mrs. Jordan. I was out of the car before she had shifted into park.

"Bye, PJ. See you tomorrow," she called as I reached around behind me to close the door.

"Thanks for the ride," I hollered as the door slammed shut. I flung my backpack over my shoulder and climbed the steps to the porch. "My English teacher," I explained to Frank, not that I thought he cared.

"I know," he answered. "Steph called a few minutes ago. She told me what happened at the hospital." He blew out a long stream of gray smoke over my head. "You okay?"

I practically dropped my backpack right there. Frank wasn't just on the porch having a cigarette. Frank was on the porch waiting for me.

"She did?"

He nodded and flicked the butt onto the lawn. "It didn't sound too good." He held the door open for me. "What's that kid got against you anyway? You sure must've pissed him off."

I shrugged my shoulders. "I dunno. He's just wacko."

"Dangerous?"

"I didn't think so. At least not until tonight."

"Drugs?"

"Yeah, something like that." This was more conversation than

Frank and I had probably had in a week. Actually, probably more than we had ever had. His curiosity made me uncomfortable.

"Hmmph," he mumbled as he closed the kitchen door behind him and flicked the switch, turning off the porch light. "Guess I had you hookin' up with the wrong guys," he said more to himself than to me.

"Huh?"

"Romano and his buddies. I thought maybe you were hangin' out with them."

Romano! I swung my backpack onto the table and started rummaging through it madly. Where was it?

"What's up? You lose something?"

"No," I blurted out quickly. "Well, yes," I confessed. Where was it? "I gotta make a phone call, Frank. I got the number somewhere."

"Phone call? Who?"

"Just somethin' I gotta do."

I dug into the pockets of my jeans. Not there. I had had those jeans on all week. What had I done with it?

I picked up my backpack and turned it upside down. Papers floated onto the floor, pens and pencils rolled across the table, an empty Mountain Dew bottle landed on a chair.

"What's goin' on, PJ?"

"A card, Frank, a little card like businesses use."

He lifted the edge of a notebook from the table and pulled out a small rectangle of stiff paper smeared with ink.

"Like this?"

Chapter Thirty-one

"Tell her I'll be here around noon," Frank said.

I nodded as I slammed the door of the pickup. Frank didn't care whether I got to school on time. Even he thought it was a good idea for me to see my mom that morning.

"Mornin', PJ. Kinda early, huh?" It was Margie. I was beginning to wonder if she lived in that little room.

"Yeah, quick stop."

I headed down the hall like a man on a mission. I was. I was stopping in just long enough to show my mom that, yes, I was still alive and just long enough to miss English class. I wasn't ready for Mrs. Jordan, or Kyle Hawkins, for that matter . . . if he was there. Yet I also didn't want to take the chance of running into Mr. Carson, so I kept my eyes open and my body moving. But,

I must admit, I would've given my right arm to know what was happening with Brian.

"PJ!"

I stopped dead in my tracks. There I was face-to-face with Taylor, Officer Taylor, in uniform. There were a whole lot of people I was worried about running into, but Taylor had not been one of them. What was he doing at the hospital? At 7:45?

"Visiting your mom?" he asked.

No, of course not. I always stop by the hospital on my way to school, just to see if there is anything I can do to help out.

"Yeah." I nodded. I was beginning to feel really hot.

"I was just stopping in to see her, too."

"Really?"

"Brian Carson confessed to being involved in her accident."

"Carson?"

"Apparently. Says he didn't mean to. I believe him."

"Carson?" I repeated. "I don't get it." I was confused. What about the dark sports car? "Wasn't it a sports car? Brian Carson owns a Jeep."

"Well, I guess a Jeep Wrangler looks pretty sporty to one of the witnesses, an older lady who—"

"—is kinda crazy," I finished for him. "Mrs. Jameson is loony. I told the other cop."

"Well, your mom's doing great, and at least we know now what happened."

The news had sunk in and I was pissed. My pain in the ass almost killed my mother.

"So . . . that makes it okay? Carson confesses? Just like that? And now it's all okay?" My voice got louder as the anger rose.

"C'mon," Taylor said quietly as he put his hand on my shoulder and turned me toward the lounge. "I think we need to talk."

Ten minutes later, I had heard the whole story. Or at least enough of the story to be totally confused. Carson's Wrangler is mistaken for a sports car? Only in Bradford. He confesses while under the influence of drugs which he's been given to calm him down because he's *on* drugs? Great medical community.

"And all this time, I thought it was—" I caught myself just in time.

"Mike Romano?"

I shrugged.

"Why not?" I answered. "Sports car and all." I paused and looked this guy straight in the eyes. "Guess I was wrong about him."

"Well, not totally."

"Huh?"

"Apparently Romano had cut Brian off just past Chapel Street. Brian was furious and took off after him. Just then your mom pulled out onto East Main. She probably misjudged how fast Brian was going. They swerved away from each other and she hit the pole. Brian panicked and kept going."

"He told you all this?"

"More or less. What he did say just let us put the pieces of the puzzle together." Taylor's voice lost its matter-of-fact, all-business tone. "I think he's really sorry, PJ."

"I think he's really an asshole," I replied.

"Well, that, too," Taylor added.

Maybe this guy was all right.

"Does my mom know?" She hadn't remembered much of anything about the accident.

"Not yet. I was on my way to talk to her when I saw you."

"Let's go tell her. I think she'd like to know it really wasn't anything she did. Not that it makes any difference, I guess."

I started to leave the lounge, but Taylor put his hand on my arm to hold me back.

"We'll do that, PJ. But first, there is one more thing."

"Yeah?"

"Thanks."

"For what?"

"Last night."

"I dunno what you're talkin' about," I mumbled. "C'mon, I gotta see my mom, and then I gotta get to school."

"Well, don't expect to see some of your classmates there."

"Yeah?"

"That's right. Three guys who've been known to cause some hassles for a lot of people aren't going to be in school here for a while."

"Yeah?" I think I was relieved. I wasn't sure.

"We got a good tip last night and caught them stealing beer and cigarettes from the Midtown Market. We're glad someone did the right thing."

"Yeah, well, that's nice, I guess."

"It *was* nice, PJ. It was. Caller ID is a wonderful thing."

Chapter Thirty-two

By the time I got to school, it was already fourth period. I hit the cafeteria even before I signed in. It wasn't my lunch period, but I was starving. Even the spongy carrots tasted pretty good. I was slurping up the last drop of milk when a female voice caught me by surprise.

"Hi, PJ. I didn't know you ate this period."

"I don't," I answered as I looked up. It was Amanda Cummings. Principal's daughter. Maybe that wasn't the right answer. "I'm not really here yet," I added.

"Huh?"

"Just got here. I went to see my mom this morning."

"Oh?" She sat down across from me. "How is she?"

"She's doin' good."

"That's nice."

Silence. I wondered if she wanted to ask me something about Billy.

"That was pretty scary about last night, wasn't it?"

My stomach tightened into a dozen knots.

"Last night?" I tried to play dumb.

"Last night . . . at Pete's . . . Mike Romano and his gang?"

"Oh, at Pete's . . . yeah . . . I guess it was a little scary."

The knots came untied. The incident at Pete's seemed light-years away. Scary? She should've been at the hospital.

"I thought they were gonna kill Henry. It's a good thing you were there."

Huh? Perhaps she had failed to see me pinned against the booth. Or Jack and his rolling pin. All I did was help Henry get back on his feet. I don't even remember her and the other girls still being there when we left.

"Yeah, sure."

"Word is those guys got arrested."

"Oh yeah?" I wondered if she noticed the rattle in my throat.

"You hadn't heard? They got caught stealing from the Market last night. I guess they're in jail or something."

"Oh yeah? No kidding."

"Figures, huh? Those guys are real losers."

"Yeah, I guess so."

Just then the bell rang for the end of the period.

"Well, I gotta go to class, PJ. See you later?" She sounded like she meant it.

"Yeah, sure." I nodded as she hopped up from the table. She stood for a couple seconds like she was about to say something more. Then she flashed a smile and wiggled the fingers of her right hand in a wave. Maybe I was wrong about Billy.

She had barely left my sight when I felt a jab in my back. I didn't need to turn around to know it was Billy's crutch.

"So?" Henry asked as he set two cafeteria trays down on the table and plopped down beside me while Billy hobbled around to the other side.

"So what?"

"What was that all about?" He was already poking at the mystery meat with his plastic fork.

"What?" I sounded defensive.

"Leave him alone." Billy sighed. "We can't all have Monicas."

"She may not be Monica, but she ain't bad." Henry was smirking.

"So where is Monica?" I asked. Henry only ate lunch with Billy and me every other day when Monica wasn't around. "She finally dump ya?"

"Gym day," he mumbled between bites of potato.

"Okay, guys, enough chick talk." Billy had finally settled into his seat. "You know anything about what happened last night, PJ? Rumors are flying everywhere."

"What kind of rumors?"

"Carson. Romano and his gang. All your favorite people."

"That was low, Jackson, low." I stabbed at my heart with my plastic fork. I thought Henry might appreciate the dramatics, but he was too busy wolfing down his food.

"Seriously, PJ, put the jokes aside. You know anything? Guys have been saying Carson's in the loony bin and Romano and Hawkins and Marston are in jail."

He was pretty close to being right on target. I poked at my apple crisp. I knew then. These guys were my friends. Who can you trust if you can't trust your friends?

I told them everything. Almost.

Chapter Thirty-three

Before the end of the day, I had made some decisions. I was going to tell Officer Taylor about the forty dollars and ask him what I should do with it. Henry said he could ask his dad what I should do. I declined the offer. Henry and I had become better friends because of this mess. I wasn't about to let Eldred Rose ruin that. Billy said I'd probably be allowed to keep it since I hadn't really done anything illegal. Part of me hoped that was true. My plan was to change the bills into quarters at the bank and dump them into the jar in the cupboard. My mom would be pleased to discover her meager attempt to save some money actually worked. She didn't need to know the truth.

I also knew Mrs. Jordan was getting her journal back. I just wasn't sure how or when. I knew it had to be before the day was over, though. If I waited until Monday, I'd lose my nerve.

All through my afternoon classes, I had practiced what I might say to her over and over in my head. "Hey, Mrs. Jordan, look what I found . . . Say, Mrs. Jordan, I'm really sorry but . . ." Hopefully, she wouldn't be in her room, and I could just leave it on her desk. Coward.

The last bell rang. I grabbed the Spanish worksheets Mrs. Stenforth was handing out and fled the room. There was no backing down.

"Hey, PJ, slow down."

I slid to a halt halfway down the hall. It was Henry. I didn't want him to know where I was going. I had told him and Billy everything about Carson going nuts at the hospital. I had told them everything I knew about Mike and Larry and Kyle. I had told them nothing about the journal.

"Did you hear? Practice is canceled."

I was glad. I had decided to stay on the team but planned on skipping practice anyway. Too many other things on my mind. Besides, I needed space from anything connected to Brian Carson.

"Yeah," Henry continued before I had a chance to answer, "the guys figure this business with Carson has put Lockwood over the deep end."

"You think he's in trouble?" I asked Henry.

"Who? Carson?"

"Lockwood. You think he's in trouble?"

Henry dropped his pack and leaned against the lockers.

"Maybe."

We stood there not looking at each other. The silence told me we were thinking the same thing. Coach Lockwood was loud and obnoxious, but he was our coach, and we knew he had good points. They were just hard to find sometimes. What we both knew was that we hoped he wasn't in trouble. Henry was the first to speak.

"You don't think he did anything, do you? I mean, Carson was clearly getting his stuff from Romano." He paused and then tapped his pack gently, two or three times, with the side of his sneaker. "You don't, do you, PJ?"

I really didn't think so. I pictured the scene in Cummings's office with Officer Taylor. Lockwood's outrage seemed genuine. If he was guilty of anything, it was being overzealous, too caught up in his team, wanting us to want to win as much as he did. But to the point of pushing Brian into taking steroids? I didn't think so. At least not intentionally.

"Nahhh," I assured Henry. "The guy's a jerk. But he's not stupid. Carson got into this mess all by himself." I rapped Henry on his arm as I swung my backpack over my shoulder and took off down the hall.

"I got a couple things I need to do," I called over my shoulder. "I'll see ya later."

"Monica and I are going to the dance tonight," he hollered after me. "You goin'?"

Dance? What dance? Who cared about a dance? Who had time to think about a dance? Besides, I hadn't ever been to a school dance. Not even with Heather.

"Probably not," I hollered to him just as I turned the corner.

Mrs. Jordan's door was open, and before I even entered the room, I could see her sitting at her desk, her head bent over something she was reading. I was well into the room before I thought that maybe I should have knocked on the door. Was she ignoring me? Maybe she hadn't heard me come in. I cleared my throat and dropped my pack onto the top of one of the desks at the front of the room. She looked up, but she didn't seem startled.

"PJ. I didn't hear you come in."

She didn't sound surprised, but she had to wonder why I was there. Picking up homework because I missed class? Not my style. Staying after to make up all the work I still owed? Hardly. Looking for extra help on an assignment? She wasn't stupid.

"Quite a night last night, wasn't it?" she said as she sat back in her chair, rolling it away slightly from the edge of her desk.

"That's sort of why I came by," I told her. "I wanted to thank you for going to see my mom and all. I think she really liked it."

"Well, I enjoyed seeing her, too. It had been a long time."

I felt stupid. I planned to give her the journal, not chat like we were friends or something. I just stood there, not knowing what to say next.

"It's too bad about Brian, isn't it?" she continued. She shook her head a little from side to side. Was she thinking about him? Feeling a little sorry for him? Maybe. But I knew even she didn't like him.

"Everyone's been buzzing about it today, but they really can't understand, can they, PJ?"

She was right. Even when I was telling Billy and Henry about what happened, I knew they had no idea what I had witnessed. Only Mrs. Jordan could understand how scary it was.

"He's going to get help, though. I think he'll be okay, in time. I was sorry, and I must admit surprised, to find out he was involved in your mother's accident."

News travels fast. But then, this is Bradford. I shrugged my shoulders. I was through being angry over that. My mother was going to be all right, and Brian Carson's life was a worse mess than I ever thought mine was. She had to know about Romano, too. Everyone knew.

"You've heard about Kyle and Larry and Mike, haven't you?" I asked her.

"Oh, yes, I have. In fact, the police were in the building today. They know now that I was in the area and that I thought I saw something. Remember? Guess it's a good thing I didn't stop to investigate. Who knows how that would've ended up?" She laughed a little. I wondered if she was picturing herself trying to stop a robbery in progress. Even I didn't see the humor in that. The laughter ended quickly, though, and she leaned forward a little. When she spoke again, she was very serious.

"And, PJ, the police know I gave you a ride home from the hospital. They may be contacting you."

I sighed deeply and shifted my weight from one foot to the other. It didn't matter. I was already involved.

"It's okay, Mrs. Jordan. Besides, I didn't really see anything happening. I don't think I'll be much help."

"Me either, PJ. They were caught with the stolen property. Apparently somebody else saw something amiss, too, and reported it."

Time to change the subject. Would Taylor keep our secret? I couldn't have everybody knowing I was a snitch. Right thing to do or not.

"I did want to thank you about my mom, but there's something else I have to do."

"Oh?" She didn't sound particularly curious, just patient.

I reached into my backpack and pulled out the blue notebook. I couldn't bring myself to look at her as I walked toward her desk and handed it to her.

"Thank you, PJ," she said quietly. "I was hoping you would find it and bring it back to me."

"I didn't take it, honest. It was with some stuff you gave me. I didn't even know I had it for a while." It was sort of the truth. I looked up at her. She was smoothing the cover with the palm of her hand. Living in my backpack for over a week had not been kind.

She looked up at me, and her eyes closed in so tightly on me that I did not dare look away.

"Did you read it?"

Doomed.

"Some."

"Just some?"

I nodded. It was the truth. I didn't read every word.

"Did you learn anything?"

I nodded. I had.

"They were private thoughts." She didn't sound angry or upset. It was just a comment. I wished she'd been angry. I would've felt better.

"I'm sorry." I was. "I should have given it right back to you when I found that I had it."

"Why didn't you?"

"I think I was afraid."

"Then I'm sorry, too, PJ."

I didn't think there was anything more to say. She sat there at her desk, and I stood waiting for an earthquake or a lightning strike or a tornado to whip through town. The world was about to end. Mrs. Jordan had nothing to say, and PJ Barnes was out of snide remarks and surly mutterings.

It was the tornado that saved us. Amanda Cummings.

"Hi, Mrs. Jordan," her voice rang out as she blew into the room. She stopped just inside the door as I turned toward her at the sound of her voice.

"Oh, sorry. I didn't mean to interrupt. I can come back later."

"No, that's okay," I muttered. "I was leaving." My face was hot, and the palms of my hands felt sticky.

"It's all right, Amanda. We were finished. What can I do for you?"

"The vocab sheet from this morning? I can't find mine. I know I got one, but I don't know what I did with it. Do you have an extra?"

"In the file sorter," Mrs. Jordan answered as she pointed toward the wall, "where they always are."

I swung my backpack over my shoulder and headed for the door.

"Oh, thanks so much," she bubbled as she bounced over to the plastic unit on the back wall that held handouts. Everyone knew that's where to find assignments and worksheets. Even me. Even if I didn't ever take any.

"You need one, PJ?" she asked, waving a sheet in the air. "You missed English this morning, didn't you?"

It was kind of nice. She was looking out for me. I stopped in the doorway.

"Yeah, I guess I do."

She handed one out to me and then placed her own neatly into a notebook she had pulled from her gym bag. I stopped and dug out a rather mangled folder and slid the sheet inside.

"Maybe we could study the words together?" she suggested. "I could use a little help." She turned to Mrs. Jordan, who was watching us from behind her desk. "You don't mind if we do the worksheet together, do you, Mrs. Jordan?"

"Not at all, Amanda. I think it's a very good idea."

"So, when shall we get together to study?" she said to me as we left the room together. "We could meet at the library, or maybe you could come over to my house."

"Tonight?" I offered cautiously.

"Tonight?" She laughed. "Not tonight. Tonight's the dance."

I guess I was going to the dance after all.

Author Marlene Carvell received a Master of Fine Arts degree from the Unversity of Texas at Austin. She has taught at both the high-school and college levels and recently retired from teaching English at a rural high school in central New York. Her first novel, Who will Tell My Brother?, received the 2003 IRA Book of the Year Award. She lives with her husband in Lebanon, New York.